THE ORDNANCE SURVEY OF THE UNITED KINGDOM

Published @ 2017 Trieste Publishing Pty Ltd

ISBN 9780649663743

The Ordnance Survey of the United Kingdom by T. Pilkington White

Except for use in any review, the reproduction or utilisation of this work in whole or in part in any form by any electronic, mechanical or other means, now known or hereafter invented, including xerography, photocopying and recording, or in any information storage or retrieval system, is forbidden without the permission of the publisher, Trieste Publishing Pty Ltd, PO Box 1576 Collingwood, Victoria 3066 Australia.

All rights reserved.

Edited by Trieste Publishing Pty Ltd.
Cover @ 2017

This book is sold subject to the condition that it shall not, by way of trade or otherwise, be lent, re-sold, hired out, or otherwise circulated without the publisher's prior consent in any form or binding or cover other than that in which it is published and without a similar condition including this condition being imposed on the subsequent purchaser.

www.triestepublishing.com

T. PILKINGTON WHITE

THE ORDNANCE SURVEY OF THE UNITED KINGDOM

THE ORDNANCE SURVEY

THE ORDNANCE SURVEY

OF THE

UNITED KINGDOM

BY

LIEUT.-COLONEL T. PILKINGTON WHITE, R.E.

(EXECUTIVE OFFICER OF THE SURVEY)

AUTHOR OF 'ARCHÆOLOGICAL SKETCHES IN SCOTLAND'

WILLIAM BLACKWOOD AND SONS
EDINBURGH AND LONDON
MDCCCLXXXVI

All Rights reserved

THE NEW YORK
PUBLIC LIBRARY
920761A
ASTOR, LENOX AND
TILDEN FOUNDATIONS
R   1937   L

TO

COLONEL RICHARD HUGH STOTHERD,

C.B., R.E.,

DIRECTOR-GENERAL OF THE ORDNANCE SURVEY,

THIS BRIEF OUTLINE OF THE HISTORY,

WORK, AND PRESENT POSITION OF

THE NATIONAL SURVEY,

IS INSCRIBED.

PREFACE.

My aim throughout these pages has been to convey to the general reader an intelligible idea of the National Survey, without overburdening them with technical details. In this sense the book is intended to be a short popular account of what might seem at first sight a dry scientific subject, suited only for experts.

The work of the Survey has hitherto been too little popularised, and if I have succeeded in making these outlines of it in any degree attractive to the public, my object will have been attained.

Some selected extracts from the contents of this volume have already appeared this year in the September number of 'Blackwood's Magazine.'

T. P. W.

ERRATUM.

Page 66, line 7 from foot, *for* " 41,614," *read* " 41,641."

CONTENTS.

CHAPTER I.

INTRODUCTION—EARLY HISTORY—ANGLO-FRENCH OPERATIONS IN 1787—PROGRESS OF SURVEY TO 1791, ... 1

CHAPTER II.

THE TRIGONOMETRICAL WORK—TRIANGULATION—SOURCES OF ERROR—COMPUTATIONS, ... 26

CHAPTER III.

NARRATIVE CONTINUED TO 1802—GEODETICAL MEASUREMENTS FOR FIGURE OF THE EARTH, ... 44

CHAPTER IV.

PROGRESS OF THE SURVEY, 1803 TO 1824—CADASTRAL SURVEY OF IRELAND—SIGNALLING, ... 60

CHAPTER V.

THE VARIOUS DESCRIPTIONS AND SCALES OF THE ORDNANCE MAPS—CONTROVERSIES ON THE SUBJECT, ... 75

CHAPTER VI.

THE MAPPING PROCESSES — NAMES — ANTIQUITIES — TREES— FOOTPATHS AND ROADS — AREAS — HYPSOMETRY — HILL-SHADING, ... 85

CHAPTER VII.

ORGANISATION OF THE SURVEY DEPARTMENT—ITS EXTRANEOUS PUBLIC SERVICES, ... 113

CHAPTER VIII.

COMPARISON OF LINEAL STANDARDS — ANGLO-FRENCH OPERATIONS IN 1861, ... 130

CHAPTER IX.

PRESENT POSITION OF THE SURVEY—ITS RECENT AUGMENTATION—ITS RELATION TO COMING LAND REFORMS, . . 141

CHAPTER X.

FUTURE OF THE ORDNANCE SURVEY—RESURVEYS—PERIODICAL REVISION OF THE MAPS—CONCLUSION, ... 159

THE ORDNANCE SURVEY OF THE UNITED KINGDOM.

CHAPTER I.

WHAT is the Ordnance Survey? how and when did it originate? what are the objects it subserves? by whom and in what manner is it executed? and who pays for it? By many it may be thought that to ask such questions at such a time as this in the history and progress of the National Survey of the United Kingdom is to imply a want of knowledge of what is going on around us altogether exceptional, and derogatory to the intelligence, or, let us say, to the most ordinary powers of observation, of the average reader. For, undoubtedly, there must be few among those resident in our islands, whether dwellers in town or country, to whom the sight of the ubiquitous Survey sapper and his belongings has not long ceased to be a novelty. His station-piles have been visible for years past on all the principal mountain-summits and hill-ranges throughout the country. Scarcely a rustic bumpkin but has gazed, and then speedily forgotten his astonishment, at the network of cross-headed poles which have sprung up in every locality, on ridges and knolls, downs and uplands, river-banks and sea-beaches, marking in succession the advance of the Ordnance Survey. The Government camping-tents and observatories have been pitched, here in a valley alongside some sheltered farmstead, there far away in the mist surmounting a rugged peak, or tied down with stays and guy-ropes to some scanty ledge hard by. The traveller along our highways must perforce, if he were not purblind, have constantly set eyes upon our altitude-marks, graven as they are along the roadsides on walls, buildings, bridges, gate-pillars, and even on the milestones. In the towns and villages the State theodolite, encased with scaffolding, has been seen perched upon the pinnacles of church steeples, on towers, domes, and monuments; or, again, in flat wooded districts oftentimes mounted on lofty portable stages to overtop the foliage. In a very short time the measuring chain will have been dragged through every county, parish, township, hamlet, and demesne throughout the land, and all the topographical features of the country, as well natural as artificial—hill and vale, river and rivulet, roads, railways, plantations, fences, buildings of every sort or size, and the like, down to such minutiæ as wells, pumps, and isolated trees in fields or hedgerows, or in towns even to the pillar post-boxes and lamp-posts along the streets—will, in exhaustive detail and with extraordinary accuracy, have been searched out and represented on the national maps.

Nevertheless, if we except certain among professional men, as civil engineers, architects, surveyors, and others, more immediately concerned with these maps, it is the fact that to the public generally their uses and value are not at all adequately known. Nay, it may be questioned if the class of gentlemen just named are those most likely to appreciate the collateral merits of our various Ordnance publications. The popular and utilitarian idea of a Government map may no doubt be a fairly correct one, as far as it goes. It will be something with which to find one's way about, or it will help us to lay out a project for a road, railway, or manufactory, gas, drainage, and water mains, telegraph lines, and so forth. But it would be altogether a mistake to suppose that these objects exhaust the information to be derived from the cartographic prints of the Cadastral Survey. The geographer, the orologist, and even the student in geology, will find in them much to instruct and interest. To the archæologist and the researcher in topographic philology, they are indispensable records, as being in a measure epitomes of the past history of the entire country, not an ancient place-name or object of antiquity escaping them. While, as for geodesy, the votaries of that science must ever acknowledge with gratitude their abiding obligations for that great completed work, the Principal Triangulation of the United Kingdom—the magnificent basis upon which the accuracy of the whole Survey rests—which has been worked out with marvellous toil, skill, and assiduity for the best part of a century past; which has involved problems of the nicest calculation, both mathematical and astronomical; has enabled us to measure with extreme exactitude meridional and longitudinal arcs, whereby approximately to ascertain the true figure of the earth; which has linked the entire series of surveyed areas covering our island into one homogeneous piece of mensuration, fixing in true relative position points over a hundred miles apart equally as the four corners of a house or any other object represented on the map, and at the same time, by a chain of triangles carried across the English Channel, connecting British with Continental geography in a scientific manner that will defy criticism to all time.

Nor can it be said that much has been contributed to current literature respecting the National Survey. I know only of two notices which have appeared in the periodicals of the day; one in a well-known quarterly, some three-and-twenty years ago — the other an excellent account, as far as it goes, by an ex-Survey officer, reprinted in 1873. There is, to be sure, the Director-General's annual report to Parliament, in the form of a blue-book, giving a *résumé* of the progress of our work from year to year; but this necessarily deals mainly with statistical information. The Department has also published several important volumes treating in detail of the various technical methods and processes adopted in its operations. And there are a large number of reports of parliamentary committees, minutes of evidence, &c., bearing upon matters connected with the Survey, which have been debated from time to time. But obviously, for the most part, these official treatises are not accessible to the general public, nor, if they were, could they be digested without a formidable amount of labour that no ordinary reader could be expected to undertake.

I propose, then, to attempt in these pages a brief sketch, with the object of bringing to light a few of the more salient points touching the early history, organisation, work, and gradual development of the Ordnance Survey, an institution embodying what is undeniably the most perfect and elaborate map-making machinery in the world, and which has evoked from foreign experts the unique encomium—"L'Ordnance Survey, œuvre sans précédent et qui devrait servir de modèle à toutes les nations civilisées."[1]

The credit of originating and carrying into execution the first tangible project for a systematic topographical survey of part of the kingdom is to be divided between two Engineer officers, both at the time holding distinguished positions on the staff of the British army. The idea would seem to have followed close upon the sanguinary termination at Culloden of the "forty-five" rebellion, and was

[1] Rapport de la Commission Militaire sur l'Exposition Universelle de 1867, p. 265. Paris: 1868.

doubtless the outcome of that unhappy rising, for it contemplated a general map of the Scottish Highlands,—precisely those parts of the country in which the heart and soul of the insurrectionary movement had all along centred. The difficulties of moving troops through these wild mountain districts, in the absence of roads, and without any clear knowledge of the passes connecting the glens and fastnesses, or of the correct distances intervening, would have been enormously lessened by the possession of good maps. Lieutenant-General Watson, an engineer, then deputy quartermaster-general to the Duke of Cumberland's forces in North Britain, appears to have taken in hand in 1747, with the assistance of some troops quartered at Fort Augustus, the survey and mapping out of the wild and inaccessible region surrounding that military post. William Roy, assistant quartermaster-general, and afterwards (1757) posted to the corps of Engineers, was, as he himself tells us in his admirable account of these early surveying operations, associated with his chief in the work. It was

General Watson, he says, who "first conceived the idea of making a map of the Highlands;" and then he proceeds: "As assistant quartermaster, it fell to my lot to begin, and afterwards to have a considerable share in the execution of that map; which, being undertaken under the auspices of the Duke of Cumberland, and meant at first to be confined to the Highlands only, was nevertheless at last extended to the Lowlands, and thus made general in what related to the mainland of Scotland, the islands (except some lesser ones near the coast) not having been surveyed." This piece of work appears to have been excellently carried out as far as it went. Roy, indeed, qualifies the result by remarking that, owing to the comparative inferiority of the instruments used, and the inadequacy of the annual grants provided for the service, "it is rather to be considered as a magnificent military sketch than a very accurate map of a country." It was interrupted by the breaking out, in 1755, of another of our then intermittent wars with France—that which gained us Canada at the cost of Wolfe

—and the work was never completed. But the seed was sown which was in due time to provide an abundant harvest.

"On the conclusion of the peace of 1763," writes General Roy, "it came for the first time under the consideration of Government to make a general survey of the whole island, at the public cost;" and the direction of this great undertaking was to have been intrusted to that officer. But, for reasons not assigned —it may have been for want of funds, inertia, procrastination, or what not — the twelve years' interval of repose enjoyed by the country before our next embroilment was allowed to pass without anything being done. With the year 1775 came the outbreak of the American War of Independence, and a further postponement of the scheme for the prosecution of the State surveys. There the matter remained in abeyance until after that severe and protracted struggle, which finally involved us in renewed hostilities with France and Spain, had been brought to a close by the peace negotiated in the first month of 1783. Meanwhile Roy, who in the interval seems to have temporarily returned to his ordinary military duties, had kept steadily in view the probable resumption of the suspended project; and already, as we have seen, well seasoned in surveying by his Scottish topographical experiences, was preparing himself to push on at the first opportunity with anything offering itself for execution in his special line. During an enforced detention in London this year (1783), he employed himself (for his own amusement, he tells us) in measuring a short base-line, about a mile and a half long, "across the fields," somewhere betwixt the parishes of Marylebone and St Pancras, to serve as a foundation for triangulating to the principal church steeples and prominent objects in the metropolis, determining their relative positions, and connecting them with the Royal Observatory at Greenwich. This work was, however, suddenly arrested by his learning that similar operations, on a more ambitious scale, were in contemplation in another quarter.

I now come to an important stage in the history of the National Surveys—namely, to negotiations for the conducting of a large and delicate trigonometrical operation, which was in reality to form the nucleus or starting-point of that elaborate system of triangulation we now possess over our islands. Early in October 1783, Comte d'Adhemar, the French ambassador at our Court, transmitted to Mr Fox a memoir, by the eminent astronomer and Academician, M. Cassini de Thury, in which were set forth the great advantages that would accrue to astronomy by carrying a series of triangles from the neighbourhood of London to Dover, and thence connecting them by observations across the English Channel with the triangulation already executed in France. The immediate object of this scheme was stated to be the more accurate ascertainment of the relative situations of the Paris and Greenwich Observatories. This memoir Mr Fox submitted to the President of the Royal Society, Sir Joseph Banks, who, towards the end of the year, consulted General Roy, and proposed he should undertake the task on the English side. Having obtained the royal sanction, the General consented.

It will be obvious that, to initiate and carry forward any network of triangles—the angles of which are to be observed, and the sides calculated by trigonometry for the purposes of an extensive terrestrial survey—the first essential is to establish a base-line in some suitable and fairly level spot, and to measure it with the utmost exactitude possible. For, inasmuch as the whole of the subsequent operations hinge upon this base, and as, moreover, to avoid undue labour and risk of inaccuracy in so nice an admeasurement, its length is necessarily made short in proportion to the length of the remaining sides of the triangulation, it is clear that a very minute error in the foundation-line will tend to multiply itself, and will affect the entire series of calculations. In the summer of the following year, then, we find the indefatigable Engineer officer hard at work on what may virtually be regarded as the first base-line of the Ordnance Survey. The site selected was on Hounslow Heath. A military working-party was furnished by the 12th Regiment of Foot, to clear the ground as a preliminary; not only, remarks Roy, because "this was obviously the most frugal method," but also for the reason "that soldiers would be more attentive to orders than country labourers." Next, the elaborate plant of the actual measuring apparatus had to be conveyed to the ground—consisting of a 100-feet coffered steel chain, specially made by Ramsden; cased glass tubing; thoroughly seasoned deal rods, in 20-feet lengths, cut out of an old Riga mast and trussed; besides a portable transit instrument, spirit-level, boring-rods and telescope, trestles, tripods, and a variety of other implements. Day after day, by slow instalments, the five miles and a fraction the line measured were covered, the contacts of every two successive rods or chain-lengths being ensured with the most minute precision; while at the same time the greatest care was taken to secure correct alignment, to adjust differences of level, to estimate variations due to temperature, and to allow for all other possible sources of error. Where each day's work left off, a fine plumb-line was suspended to mark it off—the plummet vibrating in a brass cup sunk in the ground and filled with water. It was carefully fenced round for security, and a military watch took charge of it by night, or till work was resumed. The base was measured three times — by the glass rods, the wooden rods, and the steel chain respectively. Ultimately, when remeasured in 1791, its extremities were securely marked by sinking an iron cannon underground— the centre of the bore in each case representing the exact terminal points of the line. The operation extended over two and a half months, and excited great scientific interest. The King, the Master-General of the Ordnance, and many distinguished *savants* of the day, visited the work while in progress—the President of the Royal Society giving his attendance "from morning to night in the field" during its more important stages. Altogether it was an admirably executed service, and, as we shall see further on, the three measurements tallied very closely with the result of a subsequent remeasurement. The account of the technical *modus operandi* is given in great detail, and takes up a respectable part of a good-sized volume. Such an amount of forethought and careful skill as it reveals fills one with admiration, and reflects the highest credit on the able officer who a century agone planned and accomplished it.

During the next two years the measures on the British side for the joint geodetic enterprise seem to have been maturing, and arrangements were made for the supply by the eminent opticjan already named (Ramsden) of the great 3-feet theodolite that was to be used in the operations. In the spring of 1787 the negotiations with Paris were resumed—this time through the medium of our Minister at Versailles; and a correspondence was opened between the Royal Society and the French Academy of Sciences as to the co-operation to be afforded by the latter institution in connecting the coastwise stations of the triangulation on either side of the Channel. The Academy judiciously appointed to superintend its share of the work Jean Dominic Cassini, Comte de Thury, whose memoir, as we have seen, had so strongly urged the undertaking, and who, in addition to his seventeen years' Academical membership, had recently succeeded to the distinguished post of Director of the Paris Observatory—a post which his ancestor and namesake had been the first to fill, and which had been held by successive members of this celebrated family of astronomers for upwards of a hundred years. With M. Cassini were to be associated two other commissioners, of scarcely less repute in the category of names which have made French science famous— MM. Legendre and Méchain. Méchain had been admitted to the Academical honours five years before. His skill as an observer was remarkable, and elicited a tribute from the master-geometrician Delambre; so also was the accuracy of all his calculations connected with the French Survey. Four years later, when the National Convention, having got the bit well in its teeth, was galloping away with the State coach headlong to the "Terror," that assembly had still sense enough left to sanction the employment of Delambre and Méchain, at the instance of the Academy, upon the measurement of an arc of meridian between Dunkerque and Barcelona, required for metrical purposes—though it afterwards ejected from his office and imprisoned Cassini. With the name of Adrien Marie Legendre every student of the higher mathematics must be more or less familiar; for it was he who propounded the well-known beautiful theorem which bears his name, regarding a property of what is termed in spherical trigonometry the "spherical excess." Such a contribution as this to mathematical and geodetical research would alone have sufficed to gain for its author a lasting reputation among scientists. But his labours were not few; and the services of himself and his collaborator Laplace in connection with geodesy —notably with the working out of the observations for the great French meridional arc, and the deduction therefrom of its spheroidal figure most conformable thereto—would do honour to any country.

Meantime, by the end of the summer of 1787, Roy had carried down his triangulation from the Hounslow base to the Kentish coast, in readiness for the further proceedings; and on the 23d September, the Ramsden theodolite (just completed in time) having been conveyed to Dover, he and his coadjutor, Blagden, met there the three French commissioners. A moment's pause here to note this date. Just three days earlier, the memorable and refractory Parliament of Paris, which, after its refusal to register the royal taxation edicts, had been so unceremoniously bundled off to Troyes five weeks before, had returned to the capital in triumph. Indeed, altogether this year was an eventful one in French history. Since Necker's dismissal, the finances had been going from bad to worse; and after De Fleury and D'Ormesson had given place to M. de Calonne, that suave minister of expedients was to attempt the hopeless task of arresting the State deficit, and of bolstering up the already tottering edifice of French financial credit. He had come into office towards the close of the year in which, as we have seen, the trans-Channel triangulation project was first brought to notice in England; and the story of how the Notables, convoked into unwonted session after a long abeyance, met in the month of February '87; how they would have nothing to say to his measures; how he was driven early in April to resign; how Loménie de Brienne having supplanted him, found the place equally a bed of thorns; and how, after a brief sitting, the intractable Assembly had itself to submit to dissolution,—is no new one in the annals of "la grande nation." It may, however, just serve to suggest to us—in contrast with the interesting scientific achievement which was linking the two neighbour countries at this time—the contemporary march of events on the opposite side of the water, where already the mutterings and murmurings of the great coming storm were in the air. And it may induce us to be thankful for the brief interval of peace that admitted of a reciprocal undertaking of such a kind being successfully carried out; nor should we be ungrateful to the nation which, with an exhausted exchequer, and no prospect of replenishing it, yet found the means for this and kindred work to go forward.

To resume. At Dover the party of *savants* remained two days, and then, the necessary arrangements having been concerted for the transmarine part of the observations, the Frenchmen, accompanied by Blagden, crossed over to Calais. The detailed account of the operations at this point is very interesting. On the French side, the instrument used for observing appears to have been a repeating-circle of Borda's make, about twelve inches in diameter. This description of instrument, which came into general use from this time forward with the French astronomers, had the advantages of being commodious and portable, and of diminishing errors due to defective graduation: and it would seem that Méchain formed a very high opinion of its qualities —an opinion, however, he had afterwards somewhat to modify when working out the Dunkirk - Barcelona arc. We, as already noted, made use of a splendid 3-feet theodolite by Ramsden. When the state of the weather or the long distances rendered night observations necessary, white signal-lights and reflector-lamps were flashed across the sea from the stations on either side. The joint operations continued till the 17th October, thus occupying barely a month. During the greater part of the time the weather was extremely bad: nevertheless, the particular nights on which the most important of the observations on our side were taken—namely, those from Dover Castle and Fairlight Down over to Blancnez and Montlambert on the French coast—were fortunately favourable, which, as General Roy observes, enabled the Commission "thereby to establish for ever the triangular connection between the two countries." A few of the inland stations of the triangulation still remained to be observed from; but Roy, after struggling on through the last fortnight of October, and completing all but two, encountered such tempestuous weather that, "perched on the tops of high steeples," he and his party found it impossible to proceed further till the next season, and the

Ramsden theodolite was accordingly taken down and sent off to London for the winter. On our part, the work appears to have been executed with extreme care, precision, and comparative accuracy, the angles being in some instances read as minutely as to tenths of seconds.

Scarcely was this piece of bi-national geodesy out of Roy's hands, than we find him engaged with a new base-line for verification purposes at Romney Marsh in Kent. It was nearly $5\frac{1}{2}$ miles long, and its measurement occupied a little over seven weeks, running into December 1787. In these early days of the Ordnance Survey, the advantage of military superintendence was fully recognised by the authorities, a principle which to the present time has never passed out of sight. Lieutenants Fiddes and Bryce of the Engineers assisted General Roy in the Romney Marsh operations, which presented certain difficulties owing to the ground being intersected by wide and deep ditches; and the General, after commending Fiddes for his skill, adds, that in the preliminary survey for this base, that officer had "had no other assistants than the artillerymen of his surveying party." We are also told that Major Congreve of the Artillery was intrusted with the management of the signal-lights at Shooter's Hill during the trigonometrical observations of this autumn.

Of the progress of the Ordnance Survey work during the three years following 1787, we can gather little from the official account. From Roy's two memoirs, there is evidence that the triangulation was continued into 1788, two stations in London, Primrose Hill and Hornsey Hill, being assigned to that year. But in the interval occurred the death of this accomplished officer, so entirely devoted to his work; and for the moment, as we learn from the compilers of the next record of the operations, "the further prosecution of the survey of the island seemed to expire with the General." A considerable time, we are told, elapsed after his decease without any intention on the part of the authorities of renewing the undertaking, and apparently it was not till 1791 that the work was resumed. About this time, an opportunity for acquiring a very fine theodolite of Ramsden's workmanship, similar to the one he had previously constructed for General Roy, but with some improvements, and two new steel chains by the same maker, presented itself to the Government; and the Duke of Richmond, then Master-General of the Ordnance, who seems to have taken an enlightened view of the situation, authorised their purchase, and such other steps as were necessary to proceed with the Survey.

CHAPTER II.

It may be proper here to say a few words in explanation of what is meant by a triangulation. A triangulation of a country for the purposes of a topographic or cadastral survey, is the fixation of a number of points over its area, the absolute and relative geographical position of which it is sought to determine with the greatest attainable precision the means at disposal permit. These points when joined will then form a net or congeries of triangles, within the bounds of which all the natural and artificial features that exist will be confined, and, by means of cross-lines within each triangle, be easily measured and mapped. Triangulations are sometimes undertaken for the more purely geodetic object of measuring arcs of meridian or parallel, with a view to determining the figure of the earth. In such cases the chain of triangles would form a narrow belt running north and south or east and west, as the case may be, in the general direction of the arc, though, of course, within the circuit of the belt chorographical data would be obtained, which could be utilised as for an ordinary terrestrial survey. Where the territory to be dealt with is very extensive, as on the continent of Europe, India, and the like, the triangular system is generally carried forward in strings or bands of single or double triangles, enclosing large empty polygonal spaces or loops, these interim spaces being available to be filled up at any future time. In Great Britain and Ireland, the extent of country being comparatively more limited, and the design being to execute a complete survey of the kingdom in its entirety, the method of a general web of triangles was adopted, which, beginning as we have seen with Roy's nucleus in the south-east corner of England, gradually extended itself to the farthest limits of the British Isles.

The triangulation of the Ordnance Survey may be classed under three heads—primary or principal, secondary, and minor or tertiary. In the first class are the great stations of the Survey, averaging the longest distances apart, the maximum length of side—namely, the line across the Irish Channel between Sca Fell Pike, in Cumberland, and Slieve Donard, in the county of Down—being 111 miles. These stations had to be selected with particular care and judgment to fulfil certain conditions; as that they should be reciprocally visible, and that they should form as far as practicable "well-conditioned" triangles, having sides not very unequal, the equilateral form being the best adapted to minimise the effect of incidental errors of observation. The largest-sized observing instruments, having horizontal circles of 36, 24, and 18 inches diameter, and of the highest telescopic power, were set up here; and, in consequence of the earth's curvature, it is obvious that positions thus chosen must for the most part be of commanding elevation. At many of such stations astronomical observations had to be taken to ascertain latitudes and the azimuthal bearings or inclinations of the observed lines to the true north. At thirty-two stations of the primary triangulation the latitudes were taken by means of zenith distances of certain stars with the zenith sector, and the direction of the meridian or true north bearing at the various stations was obtained from observed maximum eastern and western elongations of circumpolar stars. In the earlier days of the Ordnance Survey, Polaris was the star used for this purpose. Subsequently we observed exclusively to four stars of the constellation Ursa Minor, and to the star 51 Cephei. The latitudes and longitudes of all the principal stations were worked out geodetically with reference to the Greenwich meridian; and those of any of the other stations are similarly calculated when required. The secondary triangulation interpolates points at shorter distances apart, ranging down to five miles, the observations being made with theodolites of 12-inch circle. These triangles, again, are broken up into smaller ones, of sides from one to two miles in length, for the use of the surveyor who is to follow and measure between the stations with the chain; and a further subdivision of the trigonal spaces is made in towns, where the Survey is to be on our very large special scale. In the two last cases 7-inch instruments suffice for the measurement of the angles.

It is impossible in an account like this to give anything but the most elementary notion of the various conditions or problems involved in the working out of these triangles. It might at first sight seem a comparatively easy matter, given a base-line of a few miles to start from, to observe instrumentally from its two extremities the angles to a distant point, and, by the formulas of plane trigonometry, to calculate therefrom the lengths of the other two sides of the triangle whose apex was this point; then, upon these three lines, to push out more triangles from whose sides would spring others, and so on, thus building up an extended triangulation. And, provided the earth's surface were a plane, the difficulties in doing this would be greatly simplified. But the earth being approximately globular or spherical in shape, directly the triangles measured upon it become of a certain size, the curvature of the sides has to be taken into consideration, and we find ourselves dealing with spherical, or more properly spheroidal, triangles, whose sides are, of course, arcs of terrestrial great circles. To try and illustrate this. Suppose in a country like Holland a dead-level plain, stretching inland from the coast to an indefinite distance, at an altitude neither above nor below mean sea-level, but coincident with it. On this flat, imagine two slender Babel-like towers or columns erected, say 5000 feet high, and 60 miles apart. Having set up a theodolite on the top of one of them, and aligned out along the ground a straight course between them, conceive an imaginary curved line, parallel to or concentric with this ground-line, traced from summit to summit of the columns. Then, inasmuch as the axes of the columns although vertical are not parallel to one another, but converge to the centre of the earth, the ground-line distance from base to base, being an arc of the inner circle, must necessarily measure less than the imaginary arc of the outer circle traced between the summits. Suppose, now, a third column set up at the same height and 50 miles away from the other two, and the theodolite to have taken the subtended angles of the triangle so formed from the summit centres of all three. In such a case, the observed angles and the imaginary arcs from summit to summit would be the sides and angles of a spherical (or more strictly a spheroidal) triangle such as has to be treated in any great geodetic triangulation, when three mountain-peaks or other elevated signal-stations are connected by observations, the direct line along the ground-surface from centre to centre of the tower-bases in the illustration cited representing the true values of the trigonal arcs when projected or "reduced," as it is termed, to the mean level of the sea. In other words, the terrestrial superficies for mapping purposes is taken as what it would be were the ocean at its general level to cover the entire globe; or were the earth's land area of mountains, valleys, continents, &c., to be supposed a hollow mould or shell, underneath and into which the sea had free access. In point of fact, the three stations of a trilateral in a triangulation would generally be of unequal heights; but as, by the construction of the theodolite, the angles are reduced instrumentally to the horizontal plane at each station before being read, the illustration I have given will hold good.

In the larger triangles, then, the conditions of spherical trigonometry being brought into play, the quantity termed the "spherical excess" has to be ascertained. The figure of the earth, as already noted, is not that of a regular sphere, but of an ellipsoid or oblate spheroid, varying slightly in its ellipticity or in its radii of curvature at different points of the terrestrial surface. The determination of these variations by means of astronomical and lineal land-measurements has been one of the principal and most intricate problems of geodesy. It has been proved that the spheroidal triangles employed in a triangulation may, without appreciable error, be calculated as if they were spherical. Now, by a well-known property of all spherical triangles, the three angles of any such triangle (unlike those of a plane triangle) must exceed two right angles, or 180 degrees, the amount of this excess bearing a fixed relation to the area of the triangle and the radius of the sphere, and increasing with the size of the triangle, so that it can be approximately computed. As, however, the largest triangles practicable for observations are very small proportionally to the superficies of the hemisphere, the spherical excess does not, as a rule, amount to many seconds. It requires a triangle containing about 76 square miles — that is to say, one of 13 miles side, or thereabouts, if equilateral—to produce one second of excess. In a few of the greatest triangles it exceeded 30 seconds; and in one instance, the maximum recorded in our triangulation, it reached over 64 seconds.

The sources of error in trigonometrical observations are not few, and greatly add to the labour of the computations. In the determination of the relative altitudes of distant stations from observed vertical angles, a small correction, due to the earth's curvature, has to be applied to the apparent height of the signal-station. In the same operation an allowance has also to be made for terrestrial refraction—that is, refraction near the horizon—the effect of which, owing to irregularities of atmospheric density and temperature, is to deflect from their true direction the rays of light transmitted from the signal object to the observer's eye, and thus generally to elevate the apparent position of the object above its true position. Captain Mudge records an extraordinary instance of refraction when observing the station Glastonbury Tor from Pilsden Hill, in Dorsetshire, in June 1795, the air being exceptionally clear at the time. The unusual distinctness, he remarks, of the object (an old building on the Tor), "led me to keep my eye a long time at the telescope; and, whilst my attention was engaged, I perceived the top of the building *gradually rise* above the micrometer-wire, and so continue to do, till it was elevated 10 minutes 45 seconds above its first apparent situation. It then remained stationary, and, as night drew on, the object became indistinct. To what cause this extraordinary change in the refraction could be owing, I am at a loss to conjecture." Another aberration to be reckoned with in certain localities is the deflection of the plumb-line from verticality, due to local attraction, and caused either by the propinquity of a preponderating mass of dense matter, such as a mountain, tract of solid rock, &c., or by the presence of a corresponding deficiency, as a large cavity below the earth's surface; the result being a disturbance of the equilibrium of the earth's gravitation at that spot, and thereby of the true position of the vertical axis of the observing instrument. At Cowhythe, in Banffshire, the deflection amounted to as much as 10 seconds to the southward; at Blackdown, in Dorsetshire, to over $3\frac{1}{2}$; at Southampton, nearly $2\frac{1}{2}$ seconds,—and so on. This source of error has sometimes been very puzzling, and, it may be added, very troublesome and difficult to detect. Then there are the defects in instrumental construction, as imperfect graduation,

SOURCES OF ERROR.

eccentricity, and so forth; and there are the personal errors of the operator when using the instrument, both in its adjustments and in the readings or registry of his observations. Neither of these two last elements of faultiness and uncertainty can ever be eliminated, be the optician and observer who they may, however large and perfect the instrument, and with whatever care and precision the observations are taken. Besides the above, errors may creep in from varying phases of the signal-lights as seen by the observer, or from their not being fixed precisely over the centre of the station, and in other ways that we need not stop to particularise.

When the angles of the triangles and the other outdoor data have been obtained and recorded, the next thing is to calculate the values of the sides. The conditions of a spheroidal triangle being known, several proximate methods of working them out have been suggested, but there are three generally recognised alternative methods of procedure. The first is, having by means of the calculated spherical excess found the total error of the three observed angles, apportion this error among them, and from their corrected values as spherical angles with one of the arc-sides known, the remaining sides can be computed by the rules of spherical trigonometry. The apportionment of the error should be according to some fixed principle of the law of probabilities, whereby the most probable quantity of error, based on the number of observations of each angle, may be determined, and thus a certain "*weight*," as it is called, be attached to each. There is a rule for this, by which the reciprocals of the weights of the angles directly determine the apportionment of the error among them. We shall note a further application of this principle presently, in the method of "least squares." Formerly it was the custom either to distribute the error of the triangle equally, or to divide it in some other arbitrary way, as, for instance, on the supposed goodness of particular observations. The second way of computing the triangle is the chordal method—namely, by calculating from the spherical angles the angles subtended by the chords of the arc-sides, and obtaining the lineal measure of the chord of the known arc. The triangle to be solved then becomes a rectilinear one, and can be worked out by plane trigonometry. The third mode of solution we owe to Legendre. His ingenious and beautiful theorem, already alluded to, was in effect this: That in any spherical triangle, the sides of which are small proportionately to the radius of the sphere, if each of the angles be diminished by one-third of the spherical excess (so as to reduce their sum to two right angles), these diminished angles may be treated as those of a plane triangle having sides equal in length to the length of the spherical arc-sides straightened out into rectilinear lines. And in this way the parts of the spherical triangle can be worked out as though it were a plane triangle. It is a most handy and expeditious manner of computing—and, the conditions being just those of geodetic triangles, it can be properly applied to them; moreover, although only an approximation, it is accurate enough for all practical purposes, and has been generally adopted by geodesists. Roy and the earlier triangulators of the Ordnance Survey made use of the chordal method, but this was superseded many years ago by Legendre's principle; and the same system of calculation was employed on the great triangulation of India. "This simple and elegant method," writes one of the profoundest living geometers (of Legendre's theorem), "though of less *prima facie* accuracy than the chord method, is sufficiently near the truth for calculations of almost any degree of exactitude, and is of very easy application.[1]

From the foregoing the reader may have gathered an idea of the great difficulties to be encountered in order to ensure accuracy in the operations of any extended trigonometrical survey; but it would be impossible to convey an adequate conception of the prodigious labour and mathematical exactitude involved in the computations of the triangulation of the United Kingdom. The

[1] Account of Principal Triangulation of Great Britain and Ireland, 1858 (p. 244), drawn up by Captain (now Colonel) A. R. Clarke, R.E.

great problem was to distribute in just weight, according to systematic law, through the whole network of triangles the small angular errors we have seen to be unavoidable; and the principle on which this was effected is that known to mathematicians as the method of "least squares." It is a method grounded on the theory of probabilities, and its consideration calls in the most complicated and abstruse algebraical investigations. Not only have the three angles of each triangle to be equated or adjusted to sum 180 degrees, plus the spherical excess, but in a round of triangles constituting a polygon, the angles at the central point have each to be corrected, so that the whole may make up 360 degrees. But besides this, the several groups of polygons are mutually interdependent, forming a continuous chain, and to work them out by different routes must necessarily give varying values to the sides. These discrepancies, then, have to be treated *en bloc*, and harmonised on a system of calculation that shall minimise the probable error of the whole with the least disturbance of the original elements. Or, to put it otherwise. According to the theory of probabilities, the most probable values of the corrections to be applied to the angles of a triangulation "are those that render a minimum the sum of the squares of all the errors of observation."[1] This gives rise to a great number of what are termed "equations of condition," and the larger the extent and interlacement of the triangulation (as in Great Britain and Ireland), the greater the number of these different equations there will be to work out. Such was Bessel's application of the method of least squares to geodetical and astronomical calculations, and as employed in the computations of the great trigonometrical surveys of modern times. An approximation of it was adopted on the Ordnance Survey. It was also used in the determination of the axes of the particular spheroid which most nearly represents the surface of this country, as derived from the seventy-six equations of condition, springing out of the observed latitudes and azimuths

[1] Geodesy, by Colonel A. R. Clarke, C.B., R.E., F.R.S., &c. 1880. P. 233.

at various points of our triangulation. "In the Principal Triangulation of Great Britain and Ireland there are 218 stations, at 16 of which there are no observations; the number of observed bearings is 1554, and the number of equations of condition 920."[1] In order to avoid the solution of this enormous number of equations, containing 920 unknown quantities, "the network covering the kingdom was divided into a number of blocks, each presenting a not unmanageable number of equations of condition. . . . These calculations, all in duplicate, were completed in two years and a half—an average of eight computers being employed."[2]

I trust the reader's patience is not exhausted with these technical details. Without some little attempt to indicate them, and to make the subject intelligible, any account of the Ordnance Survey would be incomplete.

[1] Geodesy, p. 237. See also Account of Principal Triangulation of Great Britain and Ireland, p. 272.

[2] Geodesy, p. 243. "In connection," adds Clarke, "with so great a work successfully accomplished, it is but right to remark how much it was facilitated by the energy and talents of the chief computer" (of the Ordnance Survey), "Mr James O'Farrell."

CHAPTER III.

To resume, now, our review of the early operations of the Survey at the point where we digressed. In the summer of 1791, the year of recommencement of the Survey, the Hounslow base-line was remeasured by Captain William Mudge of the Artillery, colleague of Lieut.-Colonel Edward Williams, of the same regiment, upon whom Roy's mantle had fallen.[1] The result is noteworthy, as showing a remarkable agreement of all four measures — namely, by steel chain, by deal rods, by glass tubing, and, lastly, by remeasurement with the chain, —the greatest difference in any of these ad-

---

[1] In these early days of the Ordnance Survey, officers were selected to conduct it from both the Artillery and Engineer corps.

measurements being under six inches, while the length of the line exceeded five miles. In this year the triangulation was extended southward towards Fairlight and the coast, to piece in with General Roy's work; and particular attention was directed to the data for a map of Sussex, which it was intended at a future time to publish. In the narrative of the following year, we read of reflector-lamps being used of an improved kind to mark the centres of the stations for night observations, and how "the firing of the white lights was always committed to particular soldiers of the party, selected from the rest on account of their capacity and steadiness." And "at the different stations," we are told, "after the observations had been made, large stones were sunk in the ground, generally two feet under the surface, having a hole one inch square in each, whose centre was the precise point of the station." This method of marking the position of the trigonometrical points, slightly modified, has been adopted ever since on the Ordnance Survey. In 1793 the triangulating operations were continued, and observations to determine the direction of the meridian at Dunnose, in the Isle of Wight, were taken with great care in the month of April, by means of azimuths of the pole-star at its maximum apparent elongations. Similar observations were tried at Beachy Head in July; but, owing to the unsteadiness or tremulousness of the atmosphere from heat, the attempt there had to be deferred. In this and the next year, special surveys of the Hampshire coast were undertaken, and mapped on a scale of 3 inches to a mile; but these were for purely confidential military purposes.

In the summer of 1794, a highly important base of verification, nearly 7 miles long, was measured on Salisbury Plain with the steel chain. Again the labours of the Ordnance officers attracted much attention from the leaders of science,—Sir Joseph Banks, Maskelyne, astronomer-royal, and others, visiting the work during its progress. Upon this line was afterwards mainly to hang the entire triangulation of the kingdom. The length of the arc of parallel in the mean latitude between Beachy Head and Dunnose was also geometrically ascertained, in a manner presently to be described. During this and the following year, the triangulation was carried on into the counties of Dorset and Devon, and for military objects into Kent. Cornwall was reached in 1796, the principal occupation of this year being the taking of observations to determine the distance of the Siclly Isles from the Land's End, a very awkward piece of work in trigonometrical computation, owing to the unavoidable shortness of any obtainable base in the locality. This difficulty was to some extent counteracted by the circumstance that, while the party was engaged in these observations, "the air was so unusually clear, that one could sometimes, with the telescope of the great theodolite, discern the soldiers at exercise in St Mary's Island,"—a long sight to accomplish, considering that the distance of the Scilly stations from the Cornish mainland averaged nearly 30 miles. In 1798, another base-line of verification was measured at Sedgemoor, in Somersetshire, 27,680 feet, or a trifle under 5¼ miles in length; and during this and the last year of the century, the triangulation, besides being extended over Kent, was carried along the valley of the Thames, and into Essex, Suffolk, Somerset, and some of the midland counties. This year the direction of the Survey passed from Colonel Williams to Captain (afterwards Major-General) Mudge, who retained it till his death in 1820.

An especially valuable collateral result of an extended system of triangulation is the lineal terrestrial measurement of meridional arcs and of parallels for longitude between any two places in different parts of the earth's surface, and, by comparing these with the amplitudes or values of the corresponding celestial arcs obtained by astronomical observations of latitude and longitude, to infer the most probable general figure of the earth. These measurements have from early times largely occupied the attention of astronomers and scientific geographers. If, disregarding surface inequalities, our globe were a regular sphere, every great circle girding it would be a true circle, and the length of the equatorial degree of longitude and of every degree of latitude would be uniform. The celestial arch between the zeniths of any two places would then be an exact angular measure (in degrees) of the corresponding terrestrial arc; and, supposing we could with sufficient accuracy obtain the former astronomically, the latter, when turned from degrees, minutes, and seconds into feet or miles, by means of the known approximate length of the earth's diameter, would represent the veritable geodetic distance or amplitude of the arc between the places, and should agree with the same distance derived by calculation from a measured base. But, inasmuch as the earth approaches most nearly to the shape of an ellipsoid, its equatorial radius being about $13\frac{1}{2}$ miles longer than the polar semi-axis, or, according to the most recent investigations, very nearly in the proportion of $293\frac{1}{2}$ to $292\frac{1}{2}$,[1] it follows that the meridional lines

---

[1] Clarke, from the latest results up to 1880, gives the ratio as 293.465 to 292.465, and this is in close accordance with the earth's ellipticity as worked out from an entirely

are proximately ellipses, and not perfect circles. This is strictly in accordance with the ascertained geodetical fact that the degree gradually lengthens out as you proceed from the equator to the pole. On the other hand, for all practical purposes of calculation and map-projection, it has been assumed that the equator and the parallels of latitude are true circles, and that the degree of longitude, or $\frac{1}{360}$th part of the circuit of each, which would be intercepted between a number of meridian planes cutting the terrestrial surface and separated by that interval, is always the same lineal dimension.[1] The ellipticity of

distinct set of data—viz., the varying number of vibrations of a pendulum of given length in a given time in a vacuum, observed at different latitudes, and due to the force of gravitation increasing from the equator to the pole. This value of the ellipticity differs considerably from that in Airy's and Bessel's figures of the earth, but it must be remembered they had not the advantage of the completed Russian arcs, Everest's great Indian arc, the Indian longitudes, and the combined Anglo-French arc, to work from.

[1] This view has undergone modification, as from certain recent geodetical measures it has been inferred that the equator has in itself a small ellipticity. But this quantity is so small—by the last calculations only 1524 feet in a length of 7926 miles—as to be practically negligeable; and Colonel Clarke warns us that "it is necessary to guard

FIGURE OF THE EARTH.

the earth has been deduced from a variety of abstruse and laborious researches, including the investigation of astronomical phenomena, the forces of gravity, pendulum oscillations, local attraction, and the earth's mean density, in addition to geometrical admeasurements of terrestrial arcs. And the net result is this. Take an ellipse whose major and minor axes are in the ratio I have named ($293\frac{1}{2}$ to $292\frac{1}{2}$, or thereabouts), and rotate it round the shorter axis: the figure or solid thus generated, termed a solid or ellipsoid of revolution, differs very little from the form of the globe we inhabit. And this is shown to be the shape we should expect it to have taken, on the supposition that it had formerly been a fluid, or partially fluid, mass.

In the determination of this highly important and interesting problem of the figure of the earth, the arc-measurements, in various localities and in different latitudes, have been

---

against an impression that the figure of the equator is thus definitely fixed, for the available data are far too slender to warrant such a conclusion" (Geodesy—chapter "Figure of the Earth").

of the greatest service. France, Russia, Prussia, Sweden, Denmark, Hanover, Peru, South Africa, and last, but not least, India and Great Britain, have each in turn contributed a share of these invaluable factors to the investigation of the question. A consequence of the amassing of such geodetical information is this: the larger the number of the elements supplied for intercomparison, the surer our knowledge on the subject becomes; while at the same time, the results successively obtained keep modifying the conclusions previously formed from insufficient or defective data. It has been found most convenient to measure arcs nearly in the direction either of a meridian or of a parallel of latitude; and for this purpose a special triangulation with base-lines has to be undertaken, running in the general direction of the arc. The grand French arc, passing through Paris, and extending from Dunkirk to Formentera, covered over twelve degrees of latitude; the prolonged arc of the great Indian triangulation reached to nearly twenty-four degrees; while the splendid Russian arc, carried up from Bessarabia to the far north, exceeded twenty-five degrees. These were undoubtedly triumphs of geodesy.

In England, the first operation of the kind was the measurement, in 1794, for the Ordnance Survey, of a small arc of parallel between Dunnose, near Bonchurch, Isle of Wight, and Beachy Head, distant about 64 miles. The difference of longitude of the two places, and the lengths of the parallels between their meridians—or, in effect, the mean arc of parallel—were ascertained geometrically by an ingenious method of calculation, based upon the known lineal distance apart of the two stations, their respective latitudes, and their reciprocal azimuthal bearings. From these data was deduced a value for the length of a degree of parallel at each place, and also of a degree of a great circle perpendicular to the meridian, at one intermediate point nearly midway between Beachy Head and Dunnose. Since the introduction of electric telegraphy, it has become possible to observe longitudes astronomically with far greater precision than formerly; so that a comparison of the respective amplitudes of an arc of parallel, as obtained trigonometrically and by the processes of astronomy, has now become much more valuable in geodesy.

We have noted the proceedings of the British Survey down to the close of the last century. In the opening year of the new century the Survey sustained a great loss in the retirement from it of Mr Isaac Dalby, F.R.S., who had hitherto taken a leading part in all the more difficult and important branches of the work, and whose arduous labours had broken down his health. During the three years, 1800 to 1802, the main business was the measurement of a meridional arc nearly 200 miles long. The stations selected for the terminals of the arc were Dunnose, and Clifton in Yorkshire, very nearly in the same meridian—the latter lying less than a mile to westward of the former. Another convenient point chosen for an intermediate station, and still closer to the line it was intended to measure, was Arbury Hill, in Northamptonshire, something near half-way between the terminals. The object in view was a twofold one—namely, to ascertain the terrestrial distances between the points along the arc, and to check these distances by comparing them with the difference of latitude of the same points obtained astronomically. The first of these operations required the carrying forward of a chain of triangles between the two termini in the required direction; and from the already measured bases of the Survey the lengths of the sides were computed. A verification base was also measured (in 1801) near the Clifton end of the arc, at Misterton Carr, a trifle under 5 miles long. Azimuthal bearings of certain of the sides of the triangulation had also to be taken, and the direction of true north through each station to be very carefully ascertained, which was done, as in other cases, by means of observed maximum elongations of Polaris. With these bearings or angles, the computed sides, and the perpendiculars to the central meridian, the line of arc was divided into a number of parts, each representing the side of a right-angled spheroidal triangle, treated as a plane one; and thus the total lineal distance was readily worked out. This is the most usual approximate mode of arriving at the geometric or trigonometric measure of arcs of meridian.

Next there was the astronomical procedure, to obtain the celestial amplitude of the arc. To effect this, the zenith distances of a number of stars at their meridian transits were successively observed at the three stations with the fine Ramsden sector, between May and October 1802. The stars were of the constellations Perseus,[1] Draco, Cygnus, Ursa Major, and Hercules—Capella, in addition, being observed. A few observations were also taken from the Royal Observatory at Greenwich, to connect with that station. The mean of the differences between the zenith distances of each star as observed—say of Dunnose and Clifton respectively — would obviously be equivalent to the difference of the latitudes of the two places, or the astronomical amplitude of the intervening arc. Sixteen stars were made use of mutually from both terminal stations, the seconds of amplitude being read to hundredths. The total

[1] Alpha Persei was not observed from Dunnose, it would seem.

length of the arc, as obtained trigonometrically, was a trifle over 196 miles. Converting this distance into feet, and dividing by the number of seconds in the astronomical measure of the arc, would evidently give a mean value in feet to the second. Or, breaking up the arc into its component sections, the terrestrial length of any section, divided by the number of seconds in its observed celestial amplitude, supplies us with a lineal value in feet or miles of a meridional degree, whose middle point is midway between the terminals of the section — that is, in their mean latitude. The number of feet corresponding to a second on any arc of meridian in England amounts to a little over 101. It is clear, therefore, that great care in taking the astronomical observations for latitude is necessary. In the Clifton-Dunnose arc considerable disturbance was caused in the observations at the different stations by a remarkable deflection of the plumb-line, due to local attraction, and this caused some discrepancies in the work. It was unforeseen; but the results led Major Mudge to conclude there had been some error of this kind. When, afterwards, experiments were made to clear up the discrepancies, and the latitudes were taken at three other stations contiguous to Dunnose, a probable error was found of about two seconds of southerly deflection at that station, which agreed fairly well with what had been inferred in working out the original data. The arc was subsequently extended to Burleigh Moor, and more recently to the parallel of Saxavord at the northern extremity of the Shetlands, making a total distance of measured arc exceeding 706 miles (3,729,335.8 feet), or more than ten degrees of latitude. Another arc was determined between the parallel of Hensbarrow in Cornwall—one of the early stations—and Ben Hutig in the north of Sutherland. This arc measured 2,982,835½ feet, or very nearly 565 miles. The interval between the parallels passing through St Agnes Lighthouse in the Scilly Isles and the remote island of North Rona was also calculated—the distance being two yards short of 638⅓ miles. This was the second longest of all the British arcs.

The above may serve for an illustration of the principle on which meridional arcs are utilised to ascertain the varying values of the latitudinal degree, and the amount of curvature at different points on the earth's surface, whence a general figure for the terrestrial sphere best satisfying all the diverse conditions may be deduced.

CHAPTER IV.

DURING the years 1803 to 1809, the extension of the primary triangulation of the Ordnance Survey went on apace—spreading from the eastern and midland counties (Norfolk and part of Lincolnshire excepted) into Wales and across to the Isle of Man; thence through the northern counties, till nearly the whole of England was taken in; and on into Scotland along the east side, crossing the Firth of Forth to East Lomond top and Largo Law in Fife. In addition to this work, a great number of secondary and minor triangles, joining church steeples, lighthouses, signal-staves, and other conspicuous objects, were fixed from the principal stations within the same period; so that the interior surveys of the topographical details could be carried on for the general military map of England, which by this time was in regular progress, and being published on the scale of an inch to a mile. In the summer of 1806, a fresh base of verification, under 5 miles long, was measured by Colonel Mudge at Rhuddlan Marsh, near St Asaph, with steel chains and other apparatus as before—except that, unfortunately, both in this and the Misterton Carr base, oak blocks instead of iron guns were used to mark the terminal points, and these blocks have disappeared. For the next few years no great encouragement was given to the Survey. In 1811 the publication of the maps was suspended, and the number of surveyors reduced—a measure of economy that may be intelligible if we call to mind the enormous national debt the long war with France had accumulated. The triangulation of Scotland also, which had been begun in 1809, was discontinued during the three years 1810 to 1812, and again in 1820 for a short time. After the conclusion of peace, the publication of the maps was resumed; and in 1818 the gentlemen of Lincolnshire and Rutland proposed to the Government to proceed with the map of their district out of its regular turn—and this was acceded to, on condition that a portion of the cost should be locally defrayed. The object of these country gentlemen was partly to obtain a hunting-map, and partly to get the drainage of the fens marked out for reclamation purposes.

Meanwhile, and down to 1824, no large number of points were added to the great triangulation, but several of them were of the first importance, and chiefly lay in Scotland. In the remote north were Balta, Saxavord, Yell, Brassa, Fetlar, Ronas, of the Shetlands; the solitary storm-beat rocks Foula and Fair Isle; Deerness, Fitty of Westray, Stronsay, Hoy, Ronaldshay, in the Orkneys— our beacon cairns being in many instances raised among the ruined mounds and so-called "watch-towers" of a long-bygone people. In the Western Isles, Ben More in Mull, Heynish in Tiree, Tartevil in Isla, were selected; of inland Scottish mountains, Bens Lomond, Wyvis, and Hutig. Besides these, a few stations were set up in Aberdeenshire, and one or two in the southern Scotch counties. In 1817 a check base-line was measured by Captain Colby of the Engineers (afterwards Director of the Survey), assisted by Mr Gardner, chief draughtsman, on Belhelvie Links, near Aberdeen. In 1819 a military detail survey of part of the counties of Wigtown and Ayr was commenced, upon a scale of two inches to a mile, by Captain Hobbs and three subalterns of the Royal Engineers. This survey continued with diminishing numbers through the successive years from 1820 to 1827, and it extended altogether over a space of about 937 square miles. In 1823 there were seven officers of the Royal Engineers, with a small staff of assistants, employed on the Ordnance Survey.

We have now reached a point when a new departure was taken in the work of the Department, and the survey of Ireland began, a large increase in the annual money grant for Ordnance Surveys being provided for the purpose. The idea of a cadastral survey [1] of

[1] The meaning of this term has often puzzled people.

an entire country like Ireland, on so large a scale as six inches to a mile, was quite a novel one. It was the result of representations made to Government on behalf of the Irish Valuation Department, backed by petitions to Parliament and by Irish public opinion, with a view to obtaining a general survey and valuation of the town-lands throughout the island. This step had been previously recommended by successive parliamentary committees appointed to consider the subject of apportioning more equally the local burdens collected in Ireland. A bill had actually been introduced in 1819 for the valuation and survey of this part of the United Kingdom, but the measure was not persevered in.[1] Mr Spring Rice's committee, however, which

"Cadastral" or "capitastral" survey (Fr. *cadastre*), a survey and valuation of real property; Ital. *catastro;* Low Latin, *capitastrum* (from *caput*), signifying register for a poll-tax. Hence the Domesday Survey was in a sense a cadastral one, and the Ordnance Survey in its larger scales, as being the only comprehensive basis upon which a correct computation of areas and valuation of landed property for assessment of imposts is possible, may also properly be called "cadastral."

[1] *Vide* Report of Select Committee on Survey and Valuation of Ireland, 1824, p. 4.

sat in 1824, took voluminous evidence, fixed the scale and other details of the Survey, and thus gave the finishing touches to a decision which was momentous both for Ireland and ultimately for Great Britain.

The work in Ireland, including the trigonometrical operations, covered about seventeen years, being completed by 1842. The great triangulation was securely connected by transmarine lines of observation with the principal signal-stations in Great Britain, some of these lines being of great length. In 1827-28 a base of no small importance to the Survey was measured on the picturesque eastern shore of Lough Foyle, near Magilligan Point, in the county of Londonderry. It was the longest of all the base-lines in the United Kingdom, and the apparatus used in the operation was a new invention of compensation-bars, designed by Colonel Colby. The mechanism consists of a pair of parallel bars, of two different metals and different rates of expansion under heat, the two bars being connected at the centre, but otherwise freely expansible. Each such pair of bars forms a length of the apparatus, and has an ingenious automatic adjustment whereby the indicator-dots at the extremities of each length remain unaltered, notwithstanding unequal expansion or contraction of the metals at any given temperature. By this beautiful contrivance, an appreciable source of error incidental to all minutely exact measurements of distance, owing to thermometric variations of the atmosphere, is got rid of. The locality selected for the Lough Foyle base was particularly well suited for the purpose, the general level of the ground being only about 18 feet above mean sea-level. The work was done in three instalments during the summer and autumn of the two years, occupying in all sixty days, the daily progress averaging 500 feet. The total length of the line was an inch and a half under 41,614 feet, or nearly eight miles. The completion of the Irish trigonometrical work enabled us afterwards to compute geodetically the length of the arc of parallel between Valentia and Greenwich, and to compare the distance so obtained with the difference of longitude of the two places, as determined chronometrically by the Astronomer-Royal.

In 1838, the triangulation of Scotland, which had been stopped in 1823 to give place to the requirements of the Irish Survey, was resumed, and thenceforward progressed with tolerable continuity, according to the needs of the particular districts where the work was going on. The undertaking and carrying through of the six-inch survey of Ireland drew public attention to the question of the scales upon which the rest of the kingdom should be mapped. Many of the learned societies and other public bodies memorialised the Treasury on the subject; and in 1840, after consultation with the Duke of Wellington, the Board of Ordnance, and Colonel Colby, Government decided that the rest of Great Britain not yet taken up should be surveyed on the scale of six inches to the mile. Accordingly, the great counties of Lancashire and Yorkshire, and certain counties in Scotland, were produced on that scale, this work giving a marked impetus to the triangulation in those parts. In very many cases the old trigonometrical points were again observed to or from. Occasionally the exact position could not be identified; but wherever practicable, the theodolite was set up anew over the precise centre of the existing station-pile. The wooden pickets in which the frame of the instrument had rested were searched for underground, and frequently found securely wedged into deep holes sunk in the rock, and run in with lead. Sometimes the old centre-marks were intact, sometimes not. Over the marks were generally erected huge piles of stones, or of mixed turf and stones, intended to be both conspicuous and permanent objects.

The signals used on the Ordnance Survey were adapted either for day or night observations. For short distances, flagstaves and station-poles in the stone piles were sufficient. A signal-point, called the "referring object," was always set up within a mile or two of the observing station, and to this object all the angles read to the other points by the instrument were "referred." Attached to it were a pair of vertical sliding metal plates, which could be drawn apart, so as to form a narrow slit or line of light when seen against the sky. At night, a lamp was placed behind the opening to illuminate it. For long distances, it is necessary to provide some powerful illuminant at the remote signal to ensure its being visible by the observing party. Tin cones and metallic plates have been tried as sun-reflectors, but the method which has been found the simplest and best for day signalling, is an ordinary mirror or "heliostat," varying in size from circles of $3\frac{1}{2}$ to 6 and 12 inches diameter, to large rectangular frames measuring 20 by 16 inches. The adjustment of the mirror so as to reflect the solar rays in the proper direction to the observing station is ingeniously managed by setting up a small brass ring a little way from the heliostat, in line with it and the distant station, the mirror being moved about till it flashes on the ring. In this way the sunlight can be reflected so as to be visible at the very longest distances. For night-signals, Bengal or white lights were first used on the Ordnance Survey;

then Argand lamps and different kinds of powerful reflectors; and afterwards, on the Irish Survey, an improved oxy-alcoholic light of surpassing brilliancy, the invention of a Survey officer, Captain Drummond of the Engineers. Sometimes weeks went by at the camp of a "great instrument" station without the observing party once getting sight of a flash from the far-off heliostat they were watching for. To stimulate vigilance on these occasions, when to secure an observation was a matter of such paramount importance, a shrewd arrangement was contrived. "The first man that calls out 'heliostat,' when one of these star-like points shows itself, receives a shilling for his vigilance. In order to incite watchfulness in the man directing the heliostat to the observing station, and that he might miss no gleam of sunshine, a pecuniary reward was proposed in 1840 by Captain Robinson, R.E., and sanctioned by Major-General Colby, Superintendent of the Survey. The amount varied with the distance, being sixpence for each time the heliostat was observed for a distance less than 10 miles, one shilling for a distance between 10 and 20 miles, and so on; whilst for a distance between 90 and 100 miles, the allowance was fifteen shillings, and for a distance over 100 miles, a guinea."[1]

One is rather inclined to envy the workers in the old days of the great "trig.," perched, the most part of their time, on the summits of remote mountain-ranges. These men were in a sense the giants of the Survey. They had their privations to encounter, but they had also their compensations. The marvellous multiform aspects of nature so often presented to them must have been a study indeed. The lonely day and night watches —intent eyes ever on the outlook for a break in the clouds and the distant signal; the utter isolation for months from the lower world; snows and severe hailstorms at times assailing, even in early summer, the solitary camp—or furious gales, such as that which one dark night, in a wild district of Derry, blew over the men's tents, and forced Colby

[1] Account of Principal Triangulation, Ordnance Survey, p. 52.

to dismount the great theodolite ;—these episodes and experiences, notwithstanding their occasional discomforts, must, it has always seemed to me, if aught could do so, have touched the mechanical tasks of the operators with something of the gilding of the picturesque, if not the romantic, and have raised their souls for the time being above the monotony which is apt to wait upon a cut-and-dried repetition of any mere scientific detail.

The last operation in base-measuring for the Survey was carried out in 1849, when the old line of 1794 on Salisbury Plain, between Beacon Hill and Old Sarum, was re-measured with Colby's compensation-bars, as at Lough Foyle. In the earlier days of the great triangulation, the observations at the instrumental stations were for the most part personally conducted by commissioned Engineer officers; but subsequently, when the work became more extensive, experienced non-commissioned officers of Sappers were intrusted with this duty. In 1847, Major-General Thomas Frederick Colby, R.E., whose

COMPLETION OF PRIMARY TRIANGULATION. 73

eminent services to the Survey dated back to the second year of the century, and who had filled the chair of the directorate seven-and-twenty years with conspicuous ability and advantage to the State, had to retire on promotion. He was succeeded as chief of the Department by Lieut.-Colonel Hall of the Engineers, who for the next septennate occupied the post.

In 1852, the grand primary triangulation of the United Kingdom, an enterprise which had occupied between sixty and seventy years, was brought to a close. The remarkable accuracy of the results may be gathered by the reader from this one fact. When the length of the Salisbury base was *computed* from the Irish base, 350 miles distant, through the long intervening chain of triangles, this computed length differed from the measured length (as obtained from the compensation-bars) by less than five inches. And, similarly, when the Belhelvie base-line, 422 miles from Salisbury Plain, was calculated by trigonometry from the adopted mean base of the Survey, the result agreed within a few inches with the length of the line as actually chained along the ground. When all the possible sources of error in the measurements themselves, as well as in the observations and computations of a triangulation over such a wide extent of country, are taken into consideration, a nearer approach to absolute exactitude than this is scarcely conceivable; nor, if attained, would it have any practical value.

CHAPTER V.

I PASS now to the later stages of the Survey work. But to make these intelligible, it is necessary to interpolate a word as to the scales in use for the national maps. The controversy which was waged on this subject, and which began in the year when the great triangulation was completed, is now almost historic. It will be remembered there had been isolated surveys on as large a scale as six and even twenty inches to the mile very early in the progress of the National Survey; but until 1824 the scale had mainly been confined to that of one inch to a mile, primarily for the purposes of a military map. The examples, however, of France and Bavaria,—the former of which had its $\frac{1}{2500}$th, and the latter its $\frac{1}{5000}$th (or about $12\frac{1}{2}$ inches to the mile) cadastral survey,[1]—seem to have much impressed the Parliamentary Committee of 1824, and, as we have seen, the result of its deliberations was a six-inch map for the whole of Ireland. "The general tranquillity of Europe," says the Report of that Committee, "enables the State to devote the abilities and exertions of a most valuable corps of officers to an undertaking, which, though not unimportant in a military point of view, recommends itself more directly as a civil measure." Having answered so well in Ireland, the same scale was next introduced (in 1840) into the surveys of Great Britain, being intended to supersede the further preparation of the one-inch map. At this time "all England, with the exception of the six northern counties, had been surveyed on the scale of two inches, and published and engraved on the scale of one inch to a mile; and a small portion of Scotland had been previously surveyed on a

---

[1] The French cadastral plans are not, however, published and on sale, as ours are; but they are to be seen in MS. at the principal towns of the Departments or Communes.

similar scale."[1] For the next ten years the six-inch survey steadily proceeded, and such was the state of matters when the Select Committee of the House of Commons, presided over by Mr Charteris (afterwards Lord Elcho), was appointed in 1851 to investigate the question of the proper scale for Scotland, of which country only a small portion was as yet surveyed. Their recommendation was to throw over the six-inch scale, and to proceed thenceforward with the one-inch map only, — an astounding conclusion to come to, it might seem at first sight, until the conditions and circumstances under which it was reached are duly studied from the bluebooks.

This decision gave great dissatisfaction in many influential quarters, and a movement was soon set on foot to get it reversed. During the next two years, remonstrances from various public bodies poured in upon the Treasury, principally advocating the restoration of the ousted six-inch map; and a partial concession in this direction had to be made for

[1] P. iii, Report on Viscount Duncan's Committee, 1856.

the counties of Fife and Durham. A more important result followed. As early as 1837, Captain Dawson, R.E., on behalf of the Tithe Commission, had strenuously urged the adoption of a scale for survey of Great Britain corresponding to that of the French Cadastre, and in 1842 the Commission memorialised Government to that effect, Colonel Colby having also pronounced in its favour; but at that time the proposals came to nothing. When, however, in 1853, the Treasury determined to consult a large number of the most eminent scientific societies and men of science in the kingdom on the subject, an immense preponderance of opinion for a larger scale than six inches to the mile was elicited. This led to a further consultation with the same authorities, whose advice lay between a scale of 24 and $26\frac{2}{3}$ inches to a mile. The result was that a Departmental Committee, headed by Sir John Burgoyne, was appointed to consider the evidence, and this Committee recommended the adoption of an intermediate scale of $\frac{1}{2500}$ or 25.344 inches to a mile, commonly called the 25-inch scale, or one square inch to one acre.[1] This recommendation received Treasury approval in July 1854, and thus came into existence the map which has ever since been our principal parochial or rural one of the country, and which may be called the unit of the Ordnance Survey.

In the following year, the enormous scale of 126.72 inches to the mile was sanctioned for the survey of all towns with a population exceeding 4000, in lieu of the oppidan scale of 60 inches previously in use. It was at the same time decided to exclude the Scottish Highlands and extensive moorland tracts, as well as other uncultivated and thinly peopled districts, from publication on the 25-inch scale—obviously a wise decision—to save the production of reams of printed sheets

[1] This was the scale recommended by the Statistical Conference held at Brussels, under authority of the Belgian Government, in September 1853. The principal States of Europe sent delegates to this conference, and the question of national maps or *cadastres* formed one of the chief subjects of discussion. The unanimous opinion of the statists who attended the conference was in favour of this scale. It was, too, precisely that of the cadastral survey of France, which had been proposed by Laplace and Delambre to Napoleon Bonaparte, and was approved by the latter in 1804.

with little or nothing on them, for localities for which the six-inch scale was amply large enough. It was further directed that all the larger maps were to be reduced to the last-named scale, and also that the general one-inch map of the kingdom should be proceeded with as rapidly as possible. These decisions, however — and this was a very important reservation—were not to be retrospective to those parts of the country already surveyed. In June 1856 a motion adverse to the 25-inch scale was unsuccessfully raised in the Commons by Mr Edward Ellice; but a year afterwards a similar one, introduced by Sir D. Norreys, was carried by a majority of ten, the effect of which was to strike out of the estimates before Parliament the sum proposed for carrying on the 25-inch surveys. This led to the appointment of a Royal Commission, with Lord Wrottesley as chairman, which sat in May 1858, to reconsider the whole subject of the purposes, scales, progress, and prospective cost of the Ordnance Survey. This Commission confirmed generally the status in force prior to Sir D. Norreys's unfortunate resolution; but left for future determination the question of extending the $\frac{1}{2500}$th scale survey to those localities already mapped on the small one-inch scale only.

The result of all these conflicting decisions and varying orders for the prosecution of the National Survey was, as may be conceived, for the time being nothing short of disastrous, both as to economy and progress. It is only necessary to consult the evidence of the able chief of the Survey, who presided over the Department from 1854 till his retirement in 1875, Sir Henry James, to convince one's self of this. Lord Derby had, on 11th September 1858, issued a Treasury minute, sanctioning *ad interim* the continuance of the work of the Survey on the lines indicated by Lord Wrottesley's Commission, and intimating the intention of the Government to bring the matter again before Parliament. In consequence of this minute, a Select Committee of the House of Commons was nominated in 1861, "to inquire into the expediency of extending the Cadastral Survey to those portions of the United Kingdom which have been surveyed upon the scale of one inch to a mile only," and this Committee finally set at rest the much-vexed question of how the Ordnance Surveyors were to go on with their work for the future. The Committee's decision involved a large and highly important issue for the country, inasmuch as it meant nothing less than this: whether the whole of agricultural England south of Lancashire and Yorkshire, teeming with the wealth and civilisation of centuries, was to be left with little more than a road-map, perfectly useless for property or valuation purposes, while Scotland was to have, in respect of the greater part of its arable districts, a splendid *cadastre* of twenty-five times the size, and for its very bogs and lochs and barren mountains a fine map, engraved in the most minute detail, six times as large. Clearly, there could be but one conclusion for the Committee to arrive at, and for the Treasury to carry into effect. Since 1862, the Survey has been in comparatively smooth waters, and, excepting on one occasion since, when incidentally in connection with another inquiry an acceleration of our progress came on the *tapis*, parliamentary committees have troubled us no more.

Let us see, then, what are the principal classes of maps the public are now, and for a considerable time past have been, getting for their money, beginning with the maximum scale. There is (1) the town map, $\frac{1}{500}$ of the actual lineal measure of the ground, nearly 127 inches to the mile, commonly called the ten-foot map. (This has been substituted in recent years for the former five-foot town map.) There is (2) the 25-inch ($\frac{1}{2500}$) map, the true cadastral unit of the Survey. On this scale, the areas of every parcel of land are computed and published, and a square inch of the paper represents as nearly as possible one acre on the ground. We have (3) the six-inch to the mile, or what used to be termed the county map, $\frac{1}{10560}$ of actual size. And (4) comes the general, military, or geographical map of the country, on the scale of one inch to a mile ($\frac{1}{63360}$). This is the map dear to hunting men, the road or travelling map, the map for comprehensive handy purposes, from which we can best read the character of a large district of country.[1] It is produced (by engraving) in two fashions, either with or without the shading of the hill-features in relief. The reductions from the largest to all the other scales is effected by photography, in a manner and with a precision which have entirely put out of court the old methods of diminishing plans by pantograph, squares, proportional compasses, and the like. Any one, then, desiring a map of a particular town, the population of which exceeds 4000, may obtain it, according to his liking, on any of the above four scales. All these classes of maps are on sale to the public. We have, besides, an outline map, four miles, and a still smaller one of ten miles, to the inch, in hand at the present moment; the latter of which will form a sizable and compact geographical map, the very thing for schools or domestic instruction in households.

[1] "For general purposes, the map of the United Kingdom, on a scale of one inch to a mile, must, on the whole, afford the greatest amount of useful advantage to the public."—Address by Mr Edward Ryde, President of the Surveyors' Institution, 1882-83.

CHAPTER VI.

WHEN the triangulation stage of the Survey work is accomplished, the ordinary land-surveying process begins. The three vertexes of each minor triangle through the country represent points accurately fixed by the triangulation. The surveyor carefully measures the distances between them along the ground with the common Gunter's chain, and these distances are afterwards independently compared with the computed trigonometrical distances, which comparison, of course, forms a perfect test. He then breaks up the interior of the triangle with a network of cross-lines, all of which are self-checking when laid down on the paper. From these lines, which are run as nearly as may be alongside the natural and artificial features on the ground, perpendiculars are set off and measured to the bends and angles of all the surface details, fences, houses, &c. The field-books, with these measurements recorded in them, are then sent in to the respective local Survey offices, and laid down in pencil (or plotted, to use the technical term) on the squares of paper, which piece on to one another, so as to form a continuous series of plans. The outline is then copied on tracing-paper, and returned to the country for a test examination, and for the supply of all such subsidiary details as it was not the surveyor's business to furnish—*e.g.*, place and object names, antiquities, trees, and what are to constitute the ornamental adjuncts of the finished plan. The drawing of the map then follows from the completed tracings, and afterwards come the computations of the enclosure areas and the insertion of altitudes. Next, the MS. drawn plan undergoes various check processes of examination at Southampton; and, the necessary reductions to the smaller scales having meanwhile been effected, the work finally passes through the earlier publication stages into the printer's hands, and thence into the hands of the public. To trace in full the adventures of an Ordnance map, from the time when its marginal lines and trigonometrical points are scored upon it to the moment when it is deposited in the shelves of the sale-agent's shop, would be by no means without interest, were the space and the reader's patience inexhaustible; but it would mean the writing of a treatise to itself.

I cannot, however, pass over, without a special word, our system of ascertaining the local names and antiquities for record on the maps. This branch of inquiry in connection with the National Survey has ever been reckoned of the first importance. During the prosecution of the Irish Survey (1824-42), these and other collateral investigations took a far wider scope than they have done since. They included geology, natural history, botany, and economic statistics of all kinds; besides historical, philological, topographical, and archæological information. The evidence taken in 1843 before the Commission of Inquiry into the Ordnance Memoir of Ireland

—which memoir had been prepared by the officers of the Survey as a sort of guide or accompaniment to the maps—is most instructive, and reveals to us the admirable services performed side by side with the more strictly scientific labours of the trigonometrical branch, by those who then conducted the work of the Ordnance Survey. The design on which the memoir was compiled was most comprehensive. Colonel Colby told the Commission that he had directed his officers employed in Ireland to "collect information of every description which could be collected in connection with the Survey."

"Is it your idea," he is asked (Q. 277), "that the Government should accompany the Ordnance maps with a manual of useful information upon all subjects?"

"I think it would be very beneficial to the country that such a memoir should be collected. The organisation which was framed for the preparation of the Ordnance maps afforded an opportunity which never existed before of collecting information of every kind upon comparatively cheap terms."

Captain (afterwards Sir Thomas) Larcom, R.E., another Survey officer, called upon to report progress to 1843, shows us what had been done up to that date:—

"The statistic material was complete for the county of Londonderry, nearly so for Antrim, in part also for Tyrone and some other counties; but in the latter years of the Survey the interest of the officers declined, from non-publication, and very little statistical matter was collected. The historical material is much more copious. In order to ascertain the correct names of places for the engravings, that they might become a standard of orthography as well as topography, numerous maps, records, and ancient documents were examined, and copious extracts made from them. In this manner a certain amount of antiquarian information has been collected, relating to every place, parish, and town-land in Ireland—more than 70,000— and the various modes of spelling them at different times has been recorded. When these investigations were complete, it was usual to send a person thoroughly versed in the Irish language to ascertain from the old people, who still speak the language, what was the original vernacular name; and we then adopted that one among the modern modes of spelling which was most consistent with the ancient orthography, not venturing to restore the original and often obsolete name, but approaching as near to correctness as was practicable.

"Numerous drawings and characteristic sketches have also been made, and legends collected; and in these journeys, any antiquities which had been omitted were noted, and pointed out for insertion on the maps, which have thus become antiquarian as well as modern and utilitarian documents. . . .

"There have thus been collected in this branch more than 200 MS. quarto, and many smaller volumes, with several hundred plans, tracings, and drawings, together forming a treasure of located and arranged antiquarian information, which, I believe it may be safely asserted, could have been collected in no other way; while, as one of its results, the orthography of names of places in Ireland can boast the rare merit of tolerable uniformity. It has always been contemplated that the authorities for these names, and their several changes, should be published."[1]

At the Mountjoy Survey Office, Dublin, an excellent museum of specimens had by this time been formed in connection with the objects of the memoir. Larcom's proposal was not carried out. The geology and natural history branches were separated from the topographical and cartographic part of the Survey; and the publication, at Government expense, of such elaborate works as the 'Memoir on Londonderry' and the 'Report on the Geology' of the same county (by Portlock, R.E.), was discontinued. The wisdom of this decision it is not for me to dispute. Nevertheless, the undertaking of all this valuable research laid the foundation of the system upon which we have ever since compiled our MS. records, as well with respect to the nomenclature of places, natural features, and artificial objects, as to the iden-

[1] Report of Commissioners of Inquiry on Ordnance Memoir of Ireland, 1843. Appendix, p. 70.

tification and description of the antiquities of the country.

In a modified form, a descriptive name-sheet is prepared on the ground by the "examining party" for every cadastral map; each name therein is verified by reference to quoted authorities, and a resultant name is adopted. For objects of antiquarian, historical, or local interest, brief extracts from standard publications, with any local legends or particulars respecting them which have been collected, are entered in the name-sheet. The officers superintending the field-divisions of the Survey are especially charged with these inquiries, which, while of an eminently interesting nature, require at the same time considerable reading, knowledge, and discrimination to do them justice. Sir Henry James, when head of the Department, laid great stress on a personal study of these matters by his officers. He desired that they should read up the histories of their districts; and he wished them as far as practicable to take notes and sketches of the more remarkable objects of antiquity therein, these materials to be stored up in the archives of the Survey, for reference at any time when required. But, apart from what the commanding officers can do personally in this way, the mere name-sheets of themselves, as containing the designation and description of every object mapped, obviously constitute a sort of statistical memoir of every parish in the kingdom. For archæological purposes, they would be a kind of key or syllabus to the antiquities extant in the various localities at the date of survey, and one necessarily of an exhaustive character. If these documents were to be compiled with a very ordinary amount of care and labour, and then published at about cost price, I believe they would be most useful and handy guides for the study of those relics of the past, which year by year are steadily dropping away from us and passing into oblivion. I believe they would be appreciated and bought by an increasingly large class of persons of culture, who care for objects of antiquity, and want to be told where to find them without the trouble of carrying about and referring to a roll of big maps. And, with an official compilation of this kind in his hands, the student of archæology would be certain that everything antiquarian, great or small, of which there was either trace or memory remaining, was before him—everything, I say, and not, as in the case of the ordinary guide-book or county history, merely the principal or better known objects. But, meanwhile, these records exist in manuscript only; and a large mass of accumulated information goes for nothing but to register the bare name of the antiquity as it is printed (in ancient character) on our published maps.

The present Director - General (Colonel Stotherd) recently sanctioned the issue of a handbook of Instructions for the orthography of Welsh names. These instructions were compiled jointly by an eminent Welsh scholar, who acted as our referee for the place-names of the Principality, and by one of our Survey officers, a Welshman, with an intimate knowledge of the language. Similar manuals of rules are in use for some other branches of our work—*e.g.*, levelling and contouring, and field examination. The pamphlet on this latter is a really admirable compendium, embracing every detail of that most responsible duty. It was drawn up by another experienced Survey officer, and put into shape the unwritten practice of the Survey, assisted by data and suggestions from different officers and non-commissioned officers of the Department.

One of the chief safeguards upon which we rely in the Ordnance Survey for securing accuracy from first to last through all the various stages of our operations, is the system of checks and counter-checks. The work is so subdivided that the several stages form mutual tests one upon another, different men being employed in each stage. In ordinary land-surveys it is otherwise; the same individual frequently laying down his lines, plotting, drawing, and computing areas. The multiplication of checks undoubtedly tends to prevent carelessness and fraudulent practices, such as fitting in or concealing wrong work; but some have thought it has its disadvantages.

As touching the style or mode of delineation of the national maps, there are two or three special characteristics distinguishing them from the plans of ordinary surveys, which I must not omit to notice.

First, the trees. Some of the experts in surveying matters seem to have been much exercised over our representation of these features in the Ordnance maps. On all the scales larger than the one inch, not only do we show all woods, plantations, tree-clumps fenced or unfenced, orchards, and shrubberies, but also the trees along every hedgerow, scattered ornamental timber in parks, and, generally speaking, every single tree of the large or "forest" class wherever it may occur, whether in fields, by river-sides, overshadowing dwelling-houses or farmsteads, or in any other situation. Now this is undoubtedly a distinct departure from modern surveying usage, though in old estate plans there was commonly an attempt to indicate with fair accuracy the general aspect of the hedgerow trees and other timber on the estate. In our maps the single trees are delineated in correct position; but where they stand too close together, along a hedge, avenue, or elsewhere, to admit of every one being drawn on the map, in that case some of the less important ones are left out, yet still so that the proper appearance and continuity of the group of trees are maintained, and that all gaps in the row are accurately depicted. But I hear some exclaim—*Cui bono*, such elaborate arboreal representation? is this not a waste of public money for a cartographical superfluity? It has been urged that there is very little practical advantage in showing such details; that nothing is more uncertain than the continuance of timber in any given hedgerow; that improvements in agriculture frequently require the removal of the timber; that the trees often obliterate or obscure the lines on the map; and that they are difficult to erase from it afterwards in case of alterations. On the other hand, it has been pointed out that the indication of hedgerow and other isolated trees on a plan is very useful for estate and auction purposes, as this class of timber often enhances the value of a property; also, that the trees on the Ordnance maps help the engineer, or any one else using them, to find his position on the ground.

But there are wider grounds, from a national point of view, for the retention of trees on the Ordnance maps. The military element and import in all these maps must never be lost sight of. Military exigencies were the birth of the Survey; and their lien upon the work of the Department is a consideration underlying all others. It can easily be conceived that our large-scale sheets might, in the event of an invasion of the country or in times of civil disturbance, become of inestimable importance for the selection of positions of attack or defence. And it is certain that among the details which would not be a *quantité négligeable*, would figure the trees of any particular district of country. The disposition of these objects along the fences and in the open fields would be very useful information, and our six-inch map is well suited to give an officer in command of troops a perfect idea of such details. But, next, it has been well said that our maps are " public maps, and should be looked upon as records for generations to come, so that anybody consulting them in future times would know the exact character of the country at any period when they were made."[1] Let any one lay a few maps side by side, one set with and one without the trees, and then decide for himself which conveys the fuller and truer information as to the general aspect and character of the face of the country. The beauty and richness of English landscape are mainly in the trees; they are what so soften and clothe it in its unique English garb, giving it that characteristic picturesqueness that has made our land—or at least the southern part of it —in a sense the garden of the world. So that, from the artistic and æsthetic platform, the presence of the trees in the fullest detail cannot fail to be a desideratum; to say nothing of the contrast between the bare skeleton appearance of a large-scale map minus the trees, and of one of ours with them.

[1] Colonel Leach, R.E., now one of the Land Commissioners for England and Wales.—Transactions of Surveyors' Institution, 4th December 1882.

Then, again, to the arboriculturist or statistician of the natural products and features of the United Kingdom, a study of the distribution of the trees in different parts of the country would be greatly facilitated by our cadastral maps. There is yet another reason for including the trees in a survey so minute as ours, and that is, because the fundamental principle of the Ordnance Survey is to map all details or objects which are tangible features on the ground, and capable of representation on the scale of the map without overcrowding it. On the whole, then, although the views of the able president and some members of the Surveyors' Institution of London in 1882 are worthy of all respect, I must beg leave to conclude that the hedgerow and isolated trees on our maps are both an ornament and a valuable addition thereto. And it is satisfactory to find a specialist of wide experience in such matters remarking: "No one used maps more than he did, and he had not found the presence of the trees inconvenient."[1]

[1] Trans. Surveyors' Inst., 4th Dec. 1882.

Another point is the representation of footpaths across fields, &c., in the large-scale maps, and of the roads in the one-inch map. Following the consistent rule of the Survey as applied generally, our practice is to mark down on the cadastral plans all footpaths which are palpable physical features on the ground—*e.g.*, made or gravelled paths, and paths provided with stiles or foot-gates, without regard to whether they are or are not public rights-of-way. To these objects are written the letters "F.P.," denoting "footpath," in every case except when the path is very short, and there is no room for them. Yet these innocent initials are not unfrequently misunderstood, and many are the letters of inquiry addressed to Southampton on this subject by proprietors. In some cases it may be that the footpaths are private rights-of-way only; and then the sight of the path on the Ordnance map with these two obnoxious letters seems to have quite a perturbing influence on the owners. There appears to be an idea among them that the calling a footpath a footpath on our maps may hereafter be deemed to establish a title to claim it as a *public* thoroughfare. It cannot be too widely known that "F.P." means nothing more than to record the existence at the date of survey of the thing so described (to distinguish it from bridle or cart roads), of which these letters are an abbreviation; and that it is not, nor I trust ever will be, the business of the Survey to discern as to private proprietary rights, either in respect of roads and pathways, or of property boundaries as such.[1] On the one-inch map, also, when the space admits, are shown the footpaths as cross-cuts between roads; and any pedestrian who has travelled the country much will know the value of this information. Bridle-roads are distinguished from footways and carriage-roads (until lately by having the letters "B.R." attached

---

[1] The Select Committee of 1862 are very clear on this point. "They consider a map," says the Report, "the picture of the land as it exists: the boundaries set out are the material boundaries, not the boundaries of property. They could not expect that the officers of the Engineer Corps who go round the country should determine the rights of property."—Report on Cadastral Survey, 1862, p. xxii.

to them). We have recently endeavoured to meet an often expressed want in the Ordnance one-inch map, by separating roads for wheeled traffic into three categories, main and turnpike roads, ordinary metalled roads, and minor roads (including carriage-drives and cart-roads), and giving each its distinct characteristic representation on the map, either by means of a thickened line on one side, or by a difference in the width of the road on the paper, and supplemented by a small explanatory table or key on the margin of the sheet. It is hoped these additions will be recognised as an improvement, and satisfactorily meet objections that have been raised by the driving public. One thing should be remembered with regard to width of roadways (applicable also to other details) on the one-inch map: on that scale the width has necessarily to be exaggerated, in order to bring out the feature into due prominence. At the same time, the centre line of the road is always in true position.

A third point is, What is the land-surface taken in computing the acreage of fields and enclosures? If the reader has followed me in the sketch given of the trigonometrical part of the Survey work, it will be obvious that sloping fields and sinuosities in the ground can only be represented in plan by being projected to a horizontal plane, and the area on this plane of projection is the area to be calculated. In no other way could a national *cadastre* ever be fitted in within its proper geographical limits. In old days, when little else but small detached surveys were undertaken, there were approximate attempts to estimate the acreage of the actual sloping surface of the land. No doubt the content of an undulating piece of ground taken thus is somewhat larger; but the practical question is, supposing it arable, would it grow any more corn? Corn-stalks in a crop along a hillside grow upright and not perpendicular to the slope; and it is very dubitable if a farmer reaps more off the ups and downs of a field than he would if the field were level.

As to the hypsometry of the country, or, in other words, altitudes and contours. Every

Ordnance map is sprinkled over with a set of figures written to dots, generally along the roads. These represent the heights of the ground at the various points indicated by the dots. In the maps on the three larger scales, arrow-points denote where the "bench-marks" or "broad arrows" have been cut, generally two or three feet above ground-surface, upon permanent objects, and the altitude of each such mark is given to decimals of a foot (as B.M. 268.4).[1] These altitudes have been thus obtained. The great trunk roads throughout the kingdom were first spirit-levelled from a datum-point selected at the level of the sea. These formed a network of lines and cross-lines enclosing large spaces or districts, and along these lines bench-marks were fixed, their heights above the sea being afterwards computed. This was the primary or "initial levelling" of the country, accounts

[1] It should be noted that on the one-inch maps we do not show the B.M. symbol, nor the decimal in the figures of altitude, so that surface and bench-mark heights are not distinguished thereon the one from the other. It is proposed hereafter to give only surface altitudes on these maps.

of which have been compiled and published.[1] In the initial levelling of England and Wales, and most part of Scotland, the probable errors in the different lines were treated, like those of the great triangulation, by the method of least squares; and the discrepancies in the levelling along these different lines or routes, brought out in closing on common points, were dealt with as a whole, and thus equated and harmonised. The Ordnance datum-level for Great Britain—*i.e.*, the zero or starting-point—is the level of mean tide at Liverpool, as ascertained by a series of trial observations taken there by our own staff in 1844. This datum is nearly eight inches below the general mean level of the ocean round our coasts. The Ordnance datum for Ireland is not the same as for Great Britain. It is indicated by a point fixed in 1837 on Poolbeg Lighthouse in Dublin Bay, and it represented at that time the low-water mark of spring-tides. Tidal observations were made at

---

[1] Principal Lines of Spirit-Levelling in England and Wales, 1861. Do. in Scotland, 1861. Do. in Ireland, 1855.

thirty-two local stations in England, and at eighteen in Scotland, and from these the mean sea-level for both countries was obtained. A secondary system of block or district levelling has since been carried out by running branch lines off the initial ones, so as to fill up the intervening spaces. The method of levelling employed is the same, and in this way a series of heights are supplied throughout the entire country; in the cultivated districts principally along the roads—in the Highlands, both along the roads and across country, from one hill-top to another.

Besides the levels, and based upon them, we mark out on the ground and survey imaginary level lines at certain fixed intervals, beginning at 50 feet above the sea, then 100, 200, 300, and so on by steps of 100 feet to 1000 : above that, at intervals of 250 feet to the highest altitudes. These lines are technically termed "contours," or "lines of equal altitude," and are what would represent the water's edge, supposing water to stand at the various levels above named throughout the country. These contours are given on our one-inch map to the highest altitudes, and—excepting for some of the uncultivated and mountainous tracts of Scotland—also on the six-inch maps, up to 1000 feet, but not (save in a very few special cases) on any of the other scales. The procedure of the Survey, has, however, varied in this matter. In Lancashire the contours were shown on the six-inch map as close as 25 feet (vertical) apart, both in the high and low ground, and at the same interval in Yorkshire, up to the limit of 1200 feet—above that limit the Yorkshire contours were given at every 50 feet of elevation. The contours are of the greatest value to engineers and others for laying out railways, roads, canals, water-leads, drainage, &c., and for constructing ground-sections to illustrate a particular line of country. "They also form an admirable basis for hill-sketching, and for correctly expressing to the eye the surface of a country."[1] It has been objected that the Ordnance maps do not supply

[1] Letter to the Treasury from Mr Charles Vignoles, C.E. —"Correspondence on Scales and Contouring," 1854.

enough contours, or, what is the same thing, that the intervals of altitude between them are too great. The answer to this is—it is a question of cost; and more contours can at any future time be interpolated, if it is thought desirable to do so.

The shading of hill-features on our one-inch maps is another branch of work separate from and supplemental to land-surveying proper. This is undoubtedly the most beautiful and artistic of all the mapping processes of the Ordnance Survey. The *hachures* (*i.e.*, the shading lines) are first sketched in on the ground over the outline map, and then drawn fair for the engraver.[1] An electrotyped duplicate having been made from the original outline plate to receive the contours, the hill engraver graves in upon this original plate the lines which produce the exquisitely gradated shading we see upon our hill maps. The principle upon which the *hachures* are executed is, that the eye, in looking at the map,

[1] We are now utilising a recent American invention, the "air brush," to assist the hill draftsman in laying on his shades.

marvellous skill on the shaded sheets issued by the Ordnance Survey. And yet the artists were not geologists. . . . With such admirable cartographical work before them, how long will intelligent teachers continue to tolerate those antiquated monstrosities which so often do duty as wall-maps in their schoolrooms?"[1] Another accomplished geologist, writing some years ago to General Sir H. James, expresses himself thus as to our hill-shaded maps of the eastern Scottish Borders: "I never tire of looking at them; they are so beautifully done and so wonderfully suggestive. They are all the more valuable that they were constructed out of dry levellings, and without reference to geological theories." Testimony such as this is the more gratifying because it is spontaneous, and emanates from those who have no interest in belauding our work; and because it is, I think I may say, notwithstanding what a grumbler here and there may assert, undeniably true.

[1] The Physical Features of Scotland. By Professor J. Geikie, F.R.S.—Scottish Geographical Society's Magazine, January-March, 1885.

CHAPTER VII.

I PASS now to the organisation of the Ordnance Survey. This organisation rests upon a military basis, as it ever has done since the inauguration of the Department. The entire force consists of a mixed body of military men and civilians. Its traditions are military, and its discipline is largely tinged with the same element. What the primary triangulation is to the general Survey work, such is the military element to the constitution of the Survey *personnel*. It is at once the framework, the backbone, the substratum on which the stability of the whole body depends. The superintendence of the various sub-branches of the work is mainly given to the non-commissioned officers (or occasionally to the ex-non-commissioned officers) of the companies of Engineers employed on the Survey. "The headquarters of the Survey of the United Kingdom. is at Southampton. From thence all orders connected with the administration and conduct of the Survey are issued, and all the plans and maps of Great Britain are there engraved and printed; the plans and maps of Ireland are engraved and published at the Survey Office in the Phœnix Park, Dublin."[1] At Southampton the Director-General is located, and has an official residence. Here also is quartered his executive officer, who has charge of the correspondence and accounts of the Survey, and carries on, under his chief's orders, the general administrative duties of the Department. A third officer acts as assistant executive officer, regimental adjutant, and superintendent of the issue of the published maps. A fourth is in charge of the trigonometrical department (now secondary and tertiary triangulation). Two more

[1] I quote from the first detailed Report on the Survey by the Director-General, presented to Parliament as a Bluebook—1856. The status has remained unchanged.

oversee the various processes of work more immediately connected with publication—as photography, zincography, engraving, colouring the maps, and the like; while another superintends the electrotyping, workshops, and stores supply branches—these last having largely grown in importance of late years, as the out-turn and the area of the work have increased. A regimental quartermaster completes the tale of commissioned Engineer officers employed at Southampton. Until 1842, the Survey headquarters were at the Tower of London; but in consequence of the map office there having been destroyed by fire in that year, the central establishment was removed to Southampton. The Department is further divided into a number of local commands, each with a distinct central office, distributed through the country where the operations for the time being may happen to be going on. At present there are ten such divisional or field commands, all engaged in the surveying of general details, and all located in England and Wales. There is, besides, a division for Ireland, the duties of which are to revise the old six-inch survey maps of that country, to engrave the one-inch hill-maps, and to publish large-scale surveys of certain towns, besides carrying out some special services for public departments. There are also two divisions charged with the secondary levelling, the contouring, and the hill-sketching of the English work in progress; and one, with its chief office in Parliament Street, London, looks exclusively after the civil boundaries of England and Wales—county, parochial, municipal, parliamentary, and the like—so that these may be properly ascertained and mapped. Scotland, except as to the engraving of a small portion of its area, has been finished some years. Each of the above divisional units is under the chief superintendence of an officer of the Royal Engineers, assisted in some cases by a second officer belonging to the same corps. The commanding officers subdivide their men into field or office sections to suit the work they have to perform—each section being, as a rule, under the charge of a non-commissioned officer. There are four companies of Engineer

ADVANTAGES OF MILITARY ELEMENT. 117

soldiers (equivalent to a battalion) employed on the Survey, raised specially for its requirements at different times. The first to be detailed for this service was the 13th, which was formed in 1824, at the outset of the operations in Ireland. Prior to this date there were no Sapper soldiers associated with the officers of Engineers on the Ordnance Survey. In the following year two more Survey companies were raised, becoming the 14th and 16th; and in 1848 the 19th company was added to the Survey establishment. It will thus be obvious how the military constituent of the Survey leavens the whole mass. It would be impossible to overrate the advantage of having a permanent military force like this the mainstay of the business, while supplemented by civilians in larger or smaller numbers as circumstances may require. All the higher authorities have been practically agreed upon this, from the outset of the Survey to the present time. The system may be summed up epigrammatically, after the modern political fashion, as that of the three E's—combining elasticity, economy, and efficiency. And it is to be devoutly hoped that no *quasi* reformers or bureaucratic tinkers will be induced to meddle with it.

Up to 1855 the State Department under which the National Survey was conducted was the Honourable Board of Ordnance, and the directors of the Survey were immediately responsible to that Board and its Master-General. Hence its peculiar designation, "Ordnance Survey." On the abolition of that Board, the control of the Survey passed to the War Office, with which it remained till 1870, when it was transferred to H.M.'s Office of Works, and the annual vote for the Survey has since formed part of the Civil Service estimates. Thus it is that the First Commissioner of the Department of Works and Buildings is now our head, and parliamentary representative. The number of employees, military and civil, engaged on the Survey of the United Kingdom at the end of 1885, besides temporary taping-boys, was 3240. The Director-General of the Survey makes an annual report of its progress, and this report is presented to both Houses of Parliament.

And now as to the services rendered to other public departments by the Ordnance Survey. These are neither few nor unimportant, but the space already taken up in this narrative forbids more than a very meagre reference to them. In 1834 the Admiralty applied to us for secondary trigonometrical points, to enable them to lay down their coast-surveys of Cumberland and the Isle of Man. During the years 1835 to 1839, we carried forward, for the use of the Hydrographic Department of that Board, a partial secondary triangulation along the Scottish coast from Solway Firth to the Firth of Clyde. And, in a general way, there has always been a close and cordial concert between the Ordnance and Admiralty surveying departments,[1] our maps being of the greatest use to those engaged in the nautical seaboard surveys of the kingdom taking soundings; while to us, the

---

[1] See the testimony of the Hydrographer and of Sir H. James on this point in Q. 528, Minutes of Evidence before Select Committee of 1856.

Admiralty charts and large-scale drawings of special localities, such as the Wash, the estuaries of the Dee, Severn, &c., where the mud or sand flats are very extensive, afford great assistance in the delineation of the shores down to low-water mark. From 1848 to 1850, we undertook and completed for the Metropolitan Sewerage Commission a special triangulation and survey of London and eight miles round. Observatories for the theodolite were erected above the cross on the dome of St Paul's, and on the north-west tower of Westminster Abbey; and a great many levels were taken along the streets. The employment of soldiers on a work of this kind for a civil purpose was viewed in certain quarters as an objectionable innovation, and gave umbrage to some of the professional private surveyors. These formed themselves into a body called "Associated Civil Surveyors," and opposed in every way the continuance of the Sappers on this duty. Such was the hubbub raised in the matter, that the Commissioners consulted Mr Chadwick, Secretary to the Poor-Law Commission, and others, as to the expediency of allowing the Royal Engineers to go on with the service. Mr Chadwick's evidence was quoted in the 'Times' of 10th June 1848. "The example," he said, "of the employment of this corps (R.E.) on beneficial public works, qualifying them for civil employment, was worthy of public note."[1] This view carried the day, and the military were left to finish their work in peace: nor, considering the thorough way in which this work was executed, had the Commission any cause to regret their decision. A little later, we surveyed several towns on a large scale for the Board of Health. We have furnished officers and non-commissioned officers from the Survey at different times to carry out various special surveys abroad—at Jerusalem,[2] Sinai, Cyprus, the Cape, Canada,

---

[1] History of Royal Sappers and Miners.—Conolly.

[2] The Ordnance Survey of Jerusalem was undertaken in 1864-65, with War Office sanction, at the instance of the Bishop of London and other eminent persons, for certain immediate purposes connected with the sanitary improvement of the Holy City, and also to illustrate its topography. The expeditionary detachment of Engineers selected for the survey was commanded by Captain (now Sir Charles) Wilson, R.E., whose admirable work in Palestine, and sub-

British Columbia, and elsewhere. In 1858-59, when the eyes of the country were turned to fortifying the dockyards, important positions, and approaches to our principal seaports, and the great scheme for providing national defences was put forward under the auspices of a Royal Commission, it will be remembered that large sums were voted to be expended year by year upon these defences, and a great number of costly forts and batteries were erected. To meet the requirements of the War Office in connection therewith, large cadastral plans were wanted; but at that time, as the 25-inch Ordnance Survey had only recently been begun, they existed not. Hence arose a demand for special surveys on the largest scales of the selected sites and surrounding zones of country, and several localities were thus surveyed and mapped out of their turn. Special maps for Aldershot, for Chatham, for instructional purposes, for

sequent career, are well known. The party also ran a line of levels from Jaffa through Jerusalem to the Dead Sea, establishing the singular fact that the surface of this inland lake was 1298 feet below the level of the Mediterranean.

the annual Easter reviews, and suchlike, have been asked for and supplied by us at various times. These and a great many other services of a confidential nature have been rendered for the War Department by the Ordnance Survey. We have supplied maps to the Treasury. The Foreign, Colonial, and India offices have had maps from us,—maps of Turkey, maps of the Servian and Turco-Persian frontiers, maps of Afghanistan, maps of the Transvaal for a proposed railway, of Vancouver Island, of the Oregon Territory, and so on.[1] The Registrar-General's Department has laid us under contribution for the delimitation of civil boundaries, and the computation of the civil areas of the country, for the purposes of the Census returns. Her Majesty's Boundary Commissions for redistribution of seats under the several franchise bills have in each case drawn largely on our resources. Under the Reform Bill of 1832, two Engineer officers of the Survey, Lieutenants Dawson and Drummond, prepared the maps required for the Boundary Com-

[1] See the Director-General's various reports to Parliament.

mission. In 1868, six Survey officers were appointed to the Royal Commission on Parliamentary Boundaries, and assisted in holding the local inquiries. On that occasion, Sir Henry James, Director of the Survey, prepared and published for the Commissioners' Report a very large number of maps. Similarly, we were suddenly called upon under the recent Seats Bill to furnish an immense number of special maps for Sir John Lambert's Boundary Commission;[1] and a large further supply, embodying the alterations made in Committee, followed. The demand was very urgent, and we had to work extra time night and day. The total number of maps supplied for the purposes of this Commission was about 453,000. In this instance, there were six officers from the Ordnance Survey, and two ex-Survey officers, sitting either as commissioners or assistant commis-

[1] A leading article in the 'Times' of 2d March 1885 says, in reference to these maps, "The Commissioners give the credit for them to the officers of the Ordnance Survey Department, and are profuse in expressing a gratitude which every reader of the reports will feel almost equally with themselves."

sioners. In Ireland, special surveys have been made for the Irish Church Temporalities Commission; and we have for long been doing work for the Valuation Department, for the Land Judges' Court, and for the Land Commission. We have supplied special maps to the Local Government Board, and to the Stationery Office. The Geological Survey of the kingdom sends its field data to Southampton and Mountjoy, and we engrave the details on a separate set of copperplates for the use of that department. In short, most of the Government departments, and many public bodies besides those enumerated, have at one time or another come to us for assistance.

Reproduction of facsimiles of ancient MSS. by photo-zincography is another important branch of work which has fallen to us. It grew out of the discoveries of Sir H. James as to the application of photography to the copying of maps, and from the further development of the same medium by Captain de Courcy Scott, R.E., in producing carbon-print copies of maps or documents, either the same size as the originals or smaller. The first attempts at the latter process were made in 1859, and resulted early in 1860 in the production of a print of an ancient MS. deed of the time of Edward I., obtained from the Record Office; and this was considered so great a success, that the Chancellor of the Exchequer (Mr Gladstone), with the concurrence of the Master of the Rolls, authorised the Director of the Survey in the following year to undertake the reproduction and publication of facsimiles of the Cornwall part of Domesday Book. This was done by way of experiment; and the sale of the first instalment of this priceless muniment was such as to give rise to applications from the gentlemen of nearly every other county in England for copies of the remaining parts, to be similarly brought out under Government sanction. In this their lordships of the Treasury acquiesced, and thus it was that we gave to the world photo-zincographic facsimiles of that grand old descriptive survey of England, the Great and Little Domesday Books. The work is published in thirty-two volumes, and numbers in the original 1660 pages. The publication of the whole was finished by the end of 1863. It must be conceded, then, that the undertaking and successful accomplishment of such a large and laborious business as this, in the infancy of the art of photo-zincography, was no mean feat even for the Ordnance Survey.

After this followed more of the same kind of work, and we produced series after series of selected national MSS. of the highest importance, of England, Scotland, and Ireland. The original black-letter Prayer-Book of 1636 was another relic of rare interest, copied by us and published. Next appeared three volumes of Anglo-Saxon charters, the last of which has only recently come out, and embodies the invaluable collection of ancient MSS. of this class belonging to the Earl of Ashburnham, ranging in date from A.D. 694 to 1040. Transcripts from and translations of the original text have in many cases been made, and a critical commentary added to the published volumes, by a gentleman expert of her Majesty's Record Office. This eminently important editorial duty has, for some three-and-twenty years, with the permission of the Right Honourable the Master of the Rolls, been performed by Mr Basevi Sanders of that department, who has been resident in Southampton for that special purpose, and in whose custody the various ancient documents to be copied have been placed. The care, minute labour, and technical ability which have been brought to bear upon this branch of the work by Mr Sanders, it needs not for me to rehearse.

We have seen what was achieved by General Roy in the interests of science during the last century, and what was accomplished for geodesy in the way of arc-measurements towards the determination of the figure of the earth in the first years of the present century. At the hill "Arthur's Seat" in Edinburgh, in 1855, a series of very important observations were taken to ascertain the amount of deflection of the plumb-line there; and from these observations a ratio between the mean density of the mount and the mean density of the earth was calculated. And in recounting the various scientific labours of the Ordnance Survey Department, mention must not be omitted of the comparisons of the lineal standards of other countries with those of our own.

CHAPTER VIII.

In utilising the different international geodetic admeasurements to enable us to arrive at the configuration and dimensions of the earth, it is obvious that we must know the exact lengths of the several standards or units of mensuration made use of. When we say that an arc of parallel or meridian measures so many miles, or yards, or feet—so many metres or millimetres—so many toises, klafters, versts, or what not,—the first essential is to be able to express with the utmost exactitude the length of any one standard measure in terms of or relation to the others. Every measured base in the triangulation of a country must have a standard of length to which it is referred. And, inasmuch as the minutest variation in the length of a standard, say our 10-feet one set off from the national yard, would, unless allowed for, when multiplied out into a distance of several miles, and ultimately into distances of hundreds of miles, cause large and palpable errors, extreme care and nicety must be observed in determining the absolute lengths of your standards. Lineal standards are almost invariably bars made of wrought-iron, cast-steel, bronze, platinum, or some other metal. When once a good and proper national standard measure has been constructed, it becomes a national property of very high value, —it may be, to be reckoned historic in the future. Such a standard bar can of course be duplicated, the duplicate or copy being accurately compared with the original by a series of experiments, so as to test the closeness with which the two coincide at a given temperature. For, temperature being an element directly affecting all metal lineal standards, it is essential to express the length of any bar as what it is at a certain temperature—generally, for convenience, quoted at somewhere about 62° Fahrenheit; and to ascertain by a series of delicate and protracted experiments what the rate of expansion is of the particular metallic bar under different thermometric conditions.

In this way a connecting-link is established between the measures of all countries, and a common international linear value is obtained: each nation aiming to possess itself of copies of the standards of its neighbours. Prior to 1866, at the instance of Sir H. James, our Government invited the Governments of several other States to send their lineal standards to this country, with a view to an accurate intercomparison of their lengths and the lengths of our own being instituted at Southampton, where we already had a special building and apparatus erected for the purpose of such comparisons. France, Russia, Prussia, Belgium, Austria, Spain, and the United States, in addition to India, the Cape, and Australia, responded; and we were thus enabled, during the next three or four years, to carry out a series of observations of the highest importance to geodesy. The admirable and elaborate apparatus was, for the

COMPARISONS OF STANDARDS. 133

most part, designed by Captain (now Colonel) Ross Clarke, R.E., for the purposes of the tests. The several bars, with their proper lengths laid off and marked at the extremities, with the finest possible lines, visible only through the microscope, were compared in pairs in the Ordnance bar-room. The bars rest at a dead level upon an eight-roller cradle contrivance, within a box which travels smoothly along on an ingenious double carriage arrangement, and the terminals of the bars are brought under a pair of powerful micrometer microscopes entirely isolated from the former. The magnifying power of these microscopes is about 60, and the value of a division of the micrometer about one thirty-five thousandth part of an inch. There are other microscopes adjusted to test the intermediate divisions of the bars, and thermometers are placed along the latter to record the temperature. An extraordinary number of readings were taken of the micrometers and thermometers during the progress of these comparisons, and the whole were afterwards worked out into a resulting value by the method of least squares. We have two 10-feet Ordnance standard bars constructed by Troughton & Simms in 1826-27, the dimension of 10 feet having been set off at 62° Fahrenheit, and we have a 6-inch standard. These standards of our own were most carefully compared in 1844-45-46, at Southampton, with some of the earlier standards of the Survey, as General Roy's brass scale divided off into thousandths of an inch, Ramsden's prismatic bar, and others. Thus the relative lineal values of the standards were ascertained, and a connection established between the units of length employed in the earlier measured bases of the Survey and those of the later ones: the measuring rods or bars used in the bases having always been accurately compared with the standards at the time of the base-admeasurement operations. We have, besides, two copies of the standard imperial yard, one of them, marked "No. 55 Swedish Iron B,' being the particular copy which has been compared with all the geodetical standards.

There are also at Southampton our own

copies of the standard foot, the toise, and the metre. The toise is the lineal unit in which most of the European geodesic measurements are expressed; the actual original standard of this measure being the bar known as the toise of Peru. This bar was constructed in 1735 for the measurement of the arc of Peru by Bouguer and De la Condamine. The metre and the yard are both what may be termed natural measures. The first was fixed as the result of the labours of Delambre and Méchain on the Dunkirk-Montjouy arc, and purported to represent exactly the one ten-millionth part of the meridional quadrant or linear distance along a meridian from equator to pole in the northern hemisphere. This value of the metre, however, was derived from the French arc combined with the Peruvian arc, which latter the French astronomers had previously measured, a certain sphericity being assumed from these data for the intermediate parts of the quadrant. The idea of the French *savants* was to fix their metre as a decimal part of the natural geographical dimensions of the earth, and thus establish a constant standard unit of mensuration to all time. But, unfortunately, the data obtained from subsequent arc-measurements have upset this assumed value of the length of the quadrant of the Paris meridian, which now appears to be somewhat greater than ten million metres. The length of the English yard has a well-known and accurately ascertained relation to the length of the seconds pendulum, which, in the latitude of London, at the sea-level is a little over 39 inches; thus constituting an ineffaceable standard of English linear measure, depending on the law of gravitation, and reproducible as long as the terrestrial globe exists.

I have reserved to the last, mention of a most interesting and notable scientific operation, in which the Ordnance Survey took part in 1861. This was the connection of the triangulation of Great Britain with that of France, and its extension into Belgium, the former part of the work being almost a repetition of Roy's proceedings in 1787, already described. The immediate object was, by connecting the triangulation of Russia, Prussia, Austria, France, and Belgium with our own, to afford the means of computing the geometrical length of a grand arc of parallel in latitude 52°, between our station at Valentia, in the south-west of Ireland—the most westerly point of Europe—and the Russian station at Oursk, on the river Oural. Then, this length so computed could be compared with the same distance ascertained astronomically, by means of the difference of the longitude at the two stations, which the Astronomer-Royal had previously determined with the greatest precision, by the interchange of telegraphic signals. Several of the old stations of 1787 were re-established, as Fairlight and Paddlesworth on one side; and Montlambert, Gravelines, Mont-Cassel and Dunkirk on the other. Lieutenant-Colonel John Cameron,[1] then executive officer

[1] Afterwards Director-General of the Survey, in succession to Sir H. James. General Cameron's death, in 1878, deprived the Department of one who had long been intimately associated with it, and whose technical knowledge, sound judgment, and unvarying urbanity will ever be remembered by those whose privilege it was to serve under him.

of the Ordnance Survey, was given charge of the English military party: Colonel Lévret, of the Imperial Staff, superintended the French share of the undertaking. The observations were to be duplicated by the delegates of both nations, each side using precisely the same stations, and sharing the cost of erecting the necessary observatories. We made use of the old Ramsden 3-feet theodolite, and of a 24-inch and an 18-inch instrument. Our French colleagues stuck to their repeating-circles. Some fine specimens of scaffolds to carry the theodolites were erected by Mr Beaton (an ex-sergeant of Engineers), some of which were in most difficult positions, and exhibited great skill in their construction. The usual signals, including heliostats by day and reflecting-lamps by night, were made use of. We began our work on the Kentish coast in May 1861, and our observing parties crossed over to France in the summer, one or other of them remaining there from August to the end of January 1862. The weather turned very foggy and stormy towards the end of the time, and on the 10th November, at Harlettes station, the scaffold staging, 80 feet high, which had been erected by the French officers, was blown down in a very severe gale. Our Sappers, however, who were encamped there, speedily restored it. Mount Kemmel, near Ypres in Belgium, was the last station observed from by our 24-inch instrumental party; this was done towards the end of November. On the 15th March 1861, M. Thouvenel informed our ambassador (Lord Cowley) that the Préfets of the two departments of the Nord and Pas-de-Calais had been invited by the Minister of the Interior to render every assistance to our people; and the most perfect accord seems to have existed throughout this "grande opération." among all concerned.[1] An official treatise on the computations, all of which were under his immediate superintendence, was drawn up by

[1] Marshal Randon writes to M. Thouvenel: "Votre Excellence comprendra qu'il est convenable et de plus nécessaire au succès de cette grande opération, que les deux pays y participent autant que possible dans la même mesure et avec le plus parfait accord." And M. Chazot, addressing the Belgian Foreign Minister, says: "Nous efforcerons de procurer aux Ingénieurs anglais qui en seront chargés toutes les facilités désirables et le concours le plus empressé."

Captain Ross Clarke; and an excellent little account of the field-work, by Captain the Hon. le Poer Trench, R.E., is added; both these officers of the Ordnance Survey having been engaged in the joint enterprise. Such, then, was this piece of work, which in so many respects recalls Roy's skilful operation; and which, like his, reflected the highest credit on all those engaged in it. The results were most valuable, and led up to that comparison I have already alluded to, of the national lineal standards of so many Continental States with our own. Without such comparison the geometrical admeasurement of what Airy described as "probably the longest arc of parallel that man will ever measure,"[1]—an arc about 75° in length, or over a fifth of the entire circle of parallel—could never have been satisfactorily achieved.

[1] Letter to Treasury, 18th September 1860, advocating re-establishment of geodesic connection between Great Britain and the Continent.

CHAPTER IX.

As to the present position of the Survey. Great strides have been taken during the last dozen years. I have already spoken of what the arts of photography and photo-zincography have done for the work of the Department; but it would be improper to omit a word on a further special application of the latter process, which has already accomplished so much, and will undoubtedly occupy henceforward a place of the last importance in our reproductions of maps. I allude to the system we have recently adopted and perfected of producing the maps on the 6-inch scale by photo-zincographic reduction direct from the MS. 25-inch plans. Formerly the 6-inch maps were exclusively engraved on copper; but it was found that this process, so beautiful and finished in its results, was comparatively so slow that it would take a great many years, and run well into the twentieth century, before we could hope to give the public the complete map of England and Wales on that scale. This was the more serious a consideration, inasmuch as meanwhile the artificial features of the country would be changing, so that by the time many of these engraved sheets were published, the details mapped on them would be more or less obsolete. Experiments had from time to time been made with a view to apply photo-zincography to the 6-inch map as a substitute for engraving, but they were not deemed sufficiently satisfactory. So the matter rested till Major-General Cooke, the late Director-General of the Survey, succeeded in solving the difficulty. By altering our style of drawing the 25-inch plan so as to suit it for copying by the camera, and by other improvements, we are now able, after taking the reduced photographic negative of the plan, to transfer a carbon print from it, complete in every particular, to the zinc plate from which the map is to be printed. It is not too much to say that this adaptation of photography is likely to prove a lasting benefit to the Survey and to the Exchequer. To get the work done on zinc or stone in this way is incomparably cheaper than copperplate engraving, and it has the immense advantage that by it we are enabled to place a first edition (without contours) of the 6-inch map in the hands of the public a few weeks after the $\frac{1}{2500}$th plans come into Southampton from the country. The officer at present in charge of this important branch of our work and those under him are certainly to be congratulated on the perfection to which the photo-zincographed 6-inch map has been brought. Still, when all has been said and done, it can never hold a candle to the engraved map for cartographical style and finish. And for the 1-inch or smaller-scale maps, which are but slightly and at slow intervals affected by alterations of detail over the face of the country, it is to be hoped nothing will ever supersede engraving, as undoubtedly nothing is ever likely to come up to it.

Another change, which is sure to be hailed as a great boon by the purchasers of our larger-scale maps, has been introduced by the present chief of the Survey, Colonel Stotherd, with the sanction of the Treasury, although it will necessarily take some time to carry it into effect. This is the insertion of the parcel areas (as well as the reference numbers) upon the face of the printed 25-inch maps, thus dispensing with the separate area-book. And when we reflect that one of these sheets, containing 960 acres of country, and giving, in addition to surface-levels, the content of every enclosure upon it with minute accuracy, can be bought for three shillings—while a private survey of the same area would probably cost not less than seventy or eighty pounds—it will be admitted that the public get from the Ordnance Survey good value for their money.

Among other recent changes, we have introduced with great success and economy at our headquarters an electric dynamo worked by steam-power, to replace the Smee's cells previously in use, for depositing the copper in electrotyping matrixes and duplicates from the engraved copperplates. We have now forty zincographic and copperplate printing-presses continually at work here, and have recently introduced a powerful steam-press. There are an enormous number of maps of the country now on sale to the public to be produced at Southampton, as may be seen from our published catalogue, which for England and Wales alone has now grown into a huge octavo volume of 361 pages, and is constantly growing as the area under publication is enlarged. The number of maps of different sorts the Survey establishment turns out annually at Southampton is very large: in 1884 it considerably exceeded 400,000; and at the Dublin office it was over 40,000. The explanatory indexes to these maps, so necessary a key to their contents, have been very greatly improved during the last three years. In our Southampton workshops we construct for ourselves many of the surveying implements in use, such as Gunter's chains, offset and levelling staves, beam compasses, type-palettes, portable wooden houses for camping out, &c. For this purpose there are a number of lathes and machines of sorts for drilling, shaping, planing, mortising, circular-sawing, and the like, worked by steam-power. The lathes in the opticians' work-rooms, where parts of lens instruments are made or repaired, are turned by a gas-engine lately put up. A paper-cutting machine, a plate-rolling machine, and an ink-grinding mill, &c., driven by steam, have this year been added to the machinery; and we have just introduced the electric arc-light for photographic printing in winter, when the daylight is insufficient for our requirements. It is also proposed to provide the incandescent electric light for a new building, in which we cannot without detriment and risk of fire use gas. All these additions and improvements are the result of the greatly increased output of work consequent on the acceleration of the Survey, effected some five years ago; and, it is but right to add, have been very greatly facilitated by the high technical acquirements of the energetic officer, a skilled electrician and machinist, who is in charge of our "works" department. The last two years' progress of our surveying in the field is the maximum ever recorded—namely, about three million acres per annum.

I ought to add that we possess a meteorological department at our Southampton and Dublin offices, both centres ranking as stations of the second order among those of the United Kingdom. Regular daily observations are taken, and the work done has been at different times highly commended in the Reports of the Meteorological Council of the Royal Society. There is also, though now blocked out by some temporary buildings, an excellently constructed astronomical observatory at Southampton, erected in 1855. Here the old Ramsden 3-feet theodolite, a transit instrument, an 18-inch altazimuth, Colby's compensation base-measuring bars, our sidereal clock, and other apparatus, are kept. Formerly every officer, soon after joining the Survey, had to go through a short course of astronomical instruction; but within the last few years this has been discontinued, and a course of practical surveying substituted. The Ordnance Survey Library contains a very valuable collection of books on a variety of scientific subjects — including several rare and costly county histories and cognate works on local topography and archæology, — all at the disposal of the officers of the Department, to assist them in the identification of names and antiquities within their several commands, or in other ways.

As a proof of the interest manifested by other countries in the work of the British Survey, I may instance the fact that at different times officers have been sent from foreign and colonial Governments to receive instruction at the Ordnance Survey headquarters, Southampton, especially in the art of photo-zincography; indeed, nearly every European State has done this. In 1868, for example, Colonel Zimmermann of the general staff of the Prussian army, and director of their topographical department, was sent over to England to learn our organisation and methods of work; and for this purpose he visited our surveying parties both in the field and office. Colonel Stubendorf of the Russian staff, and Professor Davidson of the United States Coast Survey, visited Southampton in 1875 with a like object. At one time, also, the training of officers and men for the Indian Government caused a very frequent demand upon our resources. The Director-General of the Ordnance Survey, it may be here mentioned, is an *ex officio* honorary member of the International Goedesic Association, the permanent commission of which is presided over by General Prince Ibañez.

To bring our review of the history and work of the National Survey up to the present time, there remains only to notice the large augmentation of our force which took place in 1881, and resulted from the recommendations of the Select Committee appointed by the House of Commons to inquire into and report upon what steps should be taken "to simplify the title to land, and to facilitate the transfer thereof." This Committee was appointed in the session of 1878, and sat on till June of the following year, when it made its report. "In 1880," writes General Cooke, "the question of facilitating the transfer of land was brought prominently forward; and as a good map of the country on a sufficient scale is one of the most important desiderata for dealing successfully with that question, the attention of the country and of Parliament was called to the great desirability of completing the Ordnance Survey at an earlier date. It was therefore determined that the staff of the Survey should be about doubled, so that the work should be completed in 1890 instead of in 1900 as was previously contemplated, and the necessary steps are being taken to carry out this object."[1] Notwithstanding the difficulty of suddenly increasing so largely the strength of trained employees, it was smoothly and most successfully accomplished. And the result promises to more than justify the forecast made of the acceleration of the progress which would ensue; for we shall probably

[1] Director-General's Annual Report to Parliament on Ordnance Survey, 1881, p. 4.

be well within the pledge given to Parliament and the nation as to the completion of the Cadastral Survey of the United Kingdom in 1890, provided always that the necessary annual funds continue to be voted, and no unforeseen causes of delay arise beyond our control.

I have now endeavoured to fulfil the aim with which I set out in these pages—namely, to trace the beginnings of the National Survey, the outlines of its history, its gradual development, its organisation, its work; what it is, and what it has done for the country. To the question—in my own experience not seldom put, and by persons who ought to be better informed—What are the objects the Survey subserves? it may be well to give here a categorical answer. These principally are: (1) military, and specially for laying out the national defences; (2) geodetic; (3) geological; (4) hydrographic, as supplying accurate coast details to the nautical surveyor; (5) archæological; (6) topographic; (7) for engineering purposes of all kinds connected with the construction and maintenance of water-works, gas-works, drainage-works, telegraphs, railways, roads, canals, harbours, and so forth; (8) mineral surveys; (9) parliamentary, in reference to standing orders; (10) sanitation, as under the various Acts relating to the Public Health; (11) delimitation of the civil and ecclesiastical divisions of the country, electoral divisions, municipal, county, hundred, parochial, &c.; (12) to facilitate the adjustment of jurisdictional areas, both governmental and for local assessments, as districts under the poor-law, under school boards, under urban or rural sanitary authorities, quarter and petty sessional, assize, police, postal, and so on; (13) census and statistical information; (14) the enclosure and reclamation of waste lands; (15) registration of title; (16) simplifying and cheapening conveyances of land, deeds of sale, leases, and all transfers of landed property; (17) for miscellaneous uses of general public or private interest. This, then, though far from being an exhaustive list, is a goodly enough one to furnish forth an ample *raison d'être* for the prosecution and maintenance of a national cadastral survey.

To return to the Select Committee of 1878-79 on title and transfer of land. Nothing could be more significant than the references to the Ordnance Survey in its Report. "As regards scale and accuracy," says the Report, "the recent Cadastral Survey of England and Wales, so far as it has gone, leaves little or nothing to be desired. . . . Indeed the best testimony to the value of the 25-inch to a mile survey is furnished by the fact that, as a rule, solicitors use it wherever they can. . . . Unfortunately" (and this was true at the time) "neither the larger nor the smaller survey have been pushed forward as rapidly as could be wished. Your Committee believe that it is impossible to overrate the value of a correct official survey as a means of preventing confusion of boundaries and facilitating the identification of property, and they earnestly recommend that the important work of surveying England and Wales on both scales should be resumed and completed with as little delay as possible." And the Committee conclude their Report with certain recommendations, this being among them: "The immediate completion of the Cadastral Survey of England and Wales, and its *obligatory adoption* (subject to such modifications as may from time to time become necessary) for identifying and describing property." Coming to the minutes of evidence, we find Mr Dees (Q. 702) stating that "the Ordnance Survey is of the utmost value to every one dealing with property." But weightier still is the testimony of Lord Chancellor Cairns. (Q. 2912)—"Does not your lordship think that the pressing forward of the Ordnance Survey of 25 inches to the mile would be a great benefit to landowners, vendors, and purchasers?" "I should think very great indeed?" (2913)—"It would dispense with the necessity for any land map, would it not?" "On an extensive scale it would dispense with all estate plans, I should think." With such views as these before the Government, we can understand how it came about that the Ordnance Survey was forthwith accelerated, and the annual vote very soon more than doubled.

That this question of imminent legislative reforms, in the direction of vastly simplifying the acquisition and transfer of land, the registration of title, &c., is going to be intimately connected with the work of the Imperial Cadastral Survey, must be self-evident. It is a question entirely outside the range of party politics. It matters not what Government may be in power, the Ordnance Survey 25-inch maps, with every enclosure marked down on them and identified by a parcel area and reference number, both enfaced (as they now are) on the map itself, must become the indispensable basis of any such schemes of land reform. In an able paper contributed to the 'Fortnightly Review,' in March last year, and entitled "The Coming Land Bill," Mr C. A. Fyffe adverts to this. "There are," he says, "one or two further questions which the practical mind may be pardoned for raising in connection with registration. Are all houses in London and other towns to be registered, or only land? . . .

156   THE ORDNANCE SURVEY.

Again, on what map or survey is the registration to be based? The new 25-inch Ordnance map is one of the finest, if not the very finest, work of the kind ever executed. A landowner can, at the expense of a few shillings, purchase at the office in St Martin's Lane " (now abolished) " a map of his estate such as no conceivable private outlay could have secured for him. Every ditch, every gate, every tree by the roadside, is marked; and an area-book gives the extent of each field, corrected to the thousandth part of an acre. But this splendid work is unfortunately completed only for a small part of England.[1] For the rest, the official map is still the Tithe Survey, executed forty years ago, and so much out of date, through alterations of boundaries, enclosures, and new arrangements of fields, that it is sometimes a matter of difficulty to identify the parcels of an estate sold with the delineation of the same in the

[1] This was understating our progress, as on 31st December 1884 we had published on the 25-inch scale 26,600 square miles, not far short of one-half England and Wales. At the end of 1885 about four-sevenths of the total area of England and Wales on this scale was in the hands of the public.

Tithe Survey. . . . Now, to carry out the registration on the basis of the old antiquated Tithe Survey, when the new Ordnance map has come into existence, would be a *reductio ad absurdum* of the whole thing." The writer has here struck an important note, it may be the key-note, as to the prospective national uses of the cadastral maps of this country. Indeed one need not go beyond the sister isle to see what our maps, although these are mainly on no larger scale than six inches to the mile, have done in this direction for the community. "We are informed," says the Report of Mr Walpole's Commission on Registration of Title (1857), "by competent witnesses, that the Ordnance Survey of Ireland is considered one of the most valuable acts of practical government that has ever been carried out in Ireland. The maps are in almost universal use in the management of estates, in the sale of land, and in the valuation of land for public and private purposes." Amid the wrangle of tongues and pens, the sowing of disunion, and the general chaos of ideas abroad to-day in respect of that most unhappy country—when sentimentalists are bidding fair to make all practical government of it impossible, and their heads are being turned over the Frankenstein their folly and feebleness have created—it is something for the Survey to be able to point to a bit of firm ground like this in the muddy waters.

CHAPTER X.

AND this brings me to the conclusion of my subject—the question of the future of the Ordnance Survey, and, as indissolubly bound up with it, the question of a periodical revision of the Survey maps. The time has now arrived when the consideration of this matter can no longer be delayed. Already our surveyors have begun to fall out of work, and by the end of 1887 it is probable that the entire Cadastral Survey of the kingdom, so far as the field-surveying stage goes, will have been completed. We have now a magnificent trained staff of outdoor officials, and before they have to be discharged wholesale, it will be well to make sure that the State has no further need of their services; because, once gone, it is no easy thing to get them back again. Let us see, then, how we shall stand a year or two hence as regards work done. Ireland, the first part of the British Isles to have a comparatively large-scale survey, is, with the exception of the county of Dublin and the larger towns, mapped on no greater scale than six inches to the mile. The Irish six-inch survey was finished about 1842; but it was at first intended only to survey and map the country by town-lands, without showing subdivisions of fields—and nearly all the Ulster counties were done in this way to begin with. But it was found that for Sir Richard Griffith's general valuation of Ireland this was insufficient, and the system was changed, so as to supply the details of enclosures of land. In 1844 it was decided to go back upon the Ulster work and supplement it with the fields, and this special revision went on till its completion in 1868. A further general revision of the whole six-inch map of the island, bringing all details up to date, then began, and is still in progress. Undoubtedly a large quantity of the land in Ireland is bog or mountain waste, for which a six-inch map is ample. But that a want is felt in many instances for larger-scale maps is evidenced by the number of special surveys we have undertaken, and are still undertaking, for the purposes of the Land Judges' Court. Were a Cadastral Survey of Ireland beginning now (instead of as in 1824), there can be no sort of doubt that the cultivated country would be mapped on the 25-inch scale. Scotland has a 25-inch map of all its arable lands, excepting in the case of certain counties surveyed before Government adopted that scale. These, unluckily, are just the counties which, having been the first selected for survey, include the most valuable agricultural areas. The premier Scottish shire (Mid-Lothian), Fife, Haddington, Kirkcudbright, and Wigtown, are among them. England and Wales will have been entirely surveyed on the 25-inch scale, except mountain or very extensive moorland tracts, and — *mirabile dictu*, it might be thought—except also *Lancashire* and *Yorkshire*, which two counties were surveyed and mapped on the six-inch scale before the $\frac{1}{2500}$th cadastre was sanctioned. Here then, indeed, is an anomaly. Save London and its environs, what part of the United Kingdom can compare in industrial importance with these two northern English counties? Yet they possess (excluding the town maps) nothing larger than a six-inch survey, some parts of it upwards of forty years old, for the survey of Lancashire was executed in 1840-48, and that of Yorkshire in 1840-54. In the interval, conceive what the changes have been in the southern or manufacturing portions of these counties. Whole towns have sprung up, and probably in many cases swept away almost every vestige of the old landmarks, so that much of the face of the country would now be barely recognisable. These districts are covered with a net of new railways, old factories are gone, new ones have grown up broadcast. The moneyed interests of these great trading counties are incalculable. How much longer are they going to be content with a six-inch map, already thirty to forty years out of date, and (if we exclude one or two isolated special

25-inch surveys) without so much as a parcel area to it, when the rest of the country, much of it non-manufacturing, is rejoicing in its 25-inch map, with the area of every field and enclosure given computed to the thousandth of an acre?

Fortunately we are not without indications of the views in authoritative quarters on this subject. "The question," said Lord Bury, in a memorandum laid before the Select Committee of 1861, "of replotting Yorkshire and Lancashire, or all Ireland, on the $\frac{1}{2500}$th scale, may be well postponed till England and Wales are surveyed." Well, England and Wales are all but surveyed. But the evidence of Sir Charles Trevelyan, when Assistant Secretary to the Treasury, before Lord Duncan's Committee in 1856, is more to the point. Asked (Q. 103)—"Do you contemplate that the whole of England and Ireland should be ultimately resurveyed on the large scale of 24 inches?" (afterwards fixed at 25.344 inches), he replies: "Ultimately, after Scotland has been completed." (104)—"You would propose that Scotland should be completed upon the 24-inch scale under the reservations you have made, and that England and Ireland should afterwards be re-surveyed upon the same scale?" "That is my opinion."

But further—to pass from the particular cases just cited, where it is renewal of old surveys on a larger scale that is in question—as to the necessity of a general periodical revision of the national maps, in order to keep them up to date. From month to month, from year to year, an incessant element of change is at work upon the face of the country. It may be more here, it may be less there, but everywhere alterations are taking place. Houses are being pulled down, hedges stubbed up, fields thrown into one, old woods cleared off, waste lands brought under the plough; and new objects take their place. The additions are greater than the subtractions. In the environs of large towns, building for the most part goes on apace: in such as Liverpool, Manchester, Glasgow, Birmingham, a year or two makes an immense alteration to the cadastral map; while round about London—the survey of which was a gigantic undertaking, and lasted from 1863 to 1873, so that it is now from a dozen to twenty years old—the accessions in the way of buildings, north, south, east, and west, must be something enormous. Then, the altitude-marks cut on milestones, gate-pillars, houses, &c., are often disturbed; or subsidence may take place, so that these require occasional restoration. Then, again, the civil boundaries of the country undergo many changes in the course of years. Municipal boroughs are extended, new towns are incorporated, parliamentary boroughs are created, suppressed, or altered; divisions of counties are changed, parishes are being pared down, or added to, or amalgamated with detached parts of others by the Local Government Board, under the powers of the Divided Parishes Act. Evidently, therefore, to record all these mutations, demands a systematic correction of the cadastral maps, from time to time on the ground. The intervals at which this should be done have been variously estimated from ten to fifteen years; some have rated a longer period; but all are agreed that a regular periodical revision of the maps is a *sine quâ non*. Again let us hear the evidence of Sir C. Trevelyan, who speaks in this matter with no uncertain sound. Lord Duncan's Committee are discussing revision of the large Ordnance maps. "I contemplate," says Sir Charles (Q. 124), "a permanent staff for this purpose; I consider that it should be a permanent Government department, and I would have the maps revised from time to time. That was one of the principles laid down in the Treasury Minute of October 1840, when the six-inch scale was originally established in Great Britain." (Q. 157)—"What I understand you to say is, that in your opinion a large body of engineers will probably in future be, as it has been, in the permanent employ of the Government: you think they may be occasionally employed in revising the Ordnance Survey?"—"I go beyond that. I consider that an authentic, detailed, national survey is so important for the efficient and economical transaction of the business of this country, that even supposing we had no corps of Engineers, and no Sappers and Miners, it would still be a highly profitable employment of public money to keep up a sufficient body of experienced skilled surveyors to conduct these operations; but having a corps of scientific Engineers, and a trained and highly efficient body of Sappers and Miners, I think they may be very beneficially employed in this work; and not only will they always be available in time of war, but their military capacity and general intelligence will be much improved by the experience they have acquired in this service. That has been proved in the course of the present war." As to the extent of revision that might be looked for, this is what a very eminent civil engineer, Mr Thomas Hawksley, told Lord Bury's Committee in 1861 : " The first time upon which I used to a great extent the six-inch map was, I think, in 1846, upon the great Liverpool water-works: it was a survey which extended over 32 miles in length, and we found that map exceedingly useful; but in referring to that map since that period, I find so many changes made in the country in all parts of it, that although you do not want an entirely new survey, yet you want practically a revision already." *Already;* but this was nearly five-and-twenty years ago, and no general revision of Lancashire has taken place in the interim. Here is what the Right Hon. Edward Ellice, M.P., supported by the future Speaker of the House of Commons, Sir Evelyn (then Mr) Denison — both of whom were opposed at the time to the adoption of a Government 25-inch or "property" survey— thought thirty years since would be necessary in the way of revision of such a survey: "Your Committee," they wished to say in the Report prepared under the presidency of Lord Duncan, "upon these conflicting statements have difficulty in giving a decided opinion as to the amount of benefit to be derived from a property survey. That there would be some advantage is undeniable, but to what extent appears problematical. This point, however, is incontestable—that any lasting advantage must entirely depend upon the consent of Parliament to keep up as a permanent addition to the establishment of the country a staff of surveyors exclusively employed in the constant revision of these property plans. Such revision, involving fresh surveys, must necessarily be maintained; otherwise, looking to the never-ceasing change in the subdivision of land and disposition of buildings, from either natural or artificial causes, the plans would within a very few years become valueless as public records. They would represent as facts things that no longer existed, and would tend to mislead rather than to assist."[1] Lastly, I will quote from the official report to Parliament for 1884, by Colonel Stotherd, C.B., the present Director-General of the Ordnance Survey: " Owing to the great changes that are constantly being made by the enclosure of waste lands, erection of buildings, and other alterations in the face of the country, it will be necessary to revise the published plans periodically. . . . The revision" (a small experimental one) "of Lancashire and

[1] Report of Select Committee to the Lower House on Ordnance Survey of Scotland, 6th May 1856, p. xviii.

THE ORDNANCE SURVEY.

Yorkshire, the survey of which was made nearly forty years ago, indicates that during this period very extensive alterations have occurred, and that our present maps are, as regards the manufacturing and mining districts of those two counties, practically obsolete. . . . On the completion of the survey of England and Wales, now rapidly drawing to a close, it will be a convenient time to begin the revision, as we shall then have a trained staff of surveyors ready to commence, who, if there be no work for them, must be discharged—a proceeding it is desirable as far as possible to avoid."[1]

This question, then, of a general systematic revision of the national maps, it is for the Government and Parliament to settle, and that soon. *Nec mora nec requies.* There must be no standing still. The labours of a century have built up a magnificent edifice, the like of which no country in the world possesses, as indeed no country but our own

---

[1] His Report for 1885, published since these sheets went to press, is equally emphatic on this point. Indeed, everything possible has been done from Southampton to represent adequately the urgency of the matter.

has ever had placed in its hands in print exhaustive results of such a kind. So far the nation unquestionably owes to the Legislature and the Executive a debt of gratitude for having conceived and carried on to within measurable distance of successful accomplishment so herculean an enterprise. But John Bull must not flatter himself that the work of the Imperial Survey at home, from which he derives so many benefits, is incontinently to come to an end. He is shrewd enough to know that you cannot erect a costly structure and then leave it alone, and expend no more money on it; or launch one of the giant vessels he is so justly proud of, and expect it to float the waters for all time without ever a refit or resurvey. For a very moderate sum compared with their first cost the State maps can be kept up to date, once we can overtake the alterations which are continually taking place over the surface of the land. But a stern-chase is a long chase, and after a certain interval has been reached, every year's delay in revising the surveys drifts us further and further to leeward. Already so much of the country is in need of revision, that a considerable outlay will probably be required in the first instance—larger or smaller, according to the time it is spread over—to pull up arrears, before we can consider ourselves fairly abreast of the changes. Still, there should be no difficulty in conducting the revision in a regular and methodic manner, provided the requisite funds are forthcoming. If it is decided that the work is to cover, say, a dozen years distributed over the whole country, or, in other words, that each locality is to be corrected every twelve years, then, obviously, some such plan as the partition of the kingdom into a certain number of revisional survey districts, of which twelve is a multiple, at once suggests itself, each such district to occupy the corresponding quotient of time— one year, two years, or whatever it may be —in its rectification; and when the last of the districts has been revised, then it will be time to begin again with the first. In particular localities, of course, where building or other alterations may be going on with more than ordinary rapidity, it may be found necessary to revise oftener. A great desideratum will be that what is done in the way of revision for any given area should be done quickly, or otherwise there will be no sufficient approximation to the actual truth for the time being on any set of maps. These, however, are matters of detail which may be safely left to the proper authorities. Let them, and Parliament, and the nation, only see to it that the noble inheritance bequeathed to us by Roy and his successors is not allowed to fall into desuetude for want of timely maintenance. We have a fine State machine, in trained hands and in excellent working order: let us take care that too many of these hands are not prematurely dispersed beyond possibility of recall. We have upreared a monument of priceless scientific and practical value, which is the envy of foreign States and peoples. Let us as its custodians not grudge the means to keep it in proper order. Else, instead of being what our great Continental neighbour has been pleased to designate it— the model for all the civilised nations of the world — the Ordnance Survey will become a reproach to us, nay, nothing short of a national disgrace.

THE END.

PRINTED BY WILLIAM BLACKWOOD AND SONS.

𝔇𝔢𝔡𝔦𝔠𝔞𝔱𝔢𝔡 𝔟𝔶 𝔖𝔭𝔢𝔠𝔦𝔞𝔩 𝔓𝔢𝔯𝔪𝔦𝔰𝔰𝔦𝔬𝔫 𝔱𝔬 ℌ𝔢𝔯 ℜ𝔬𝔶𝔞𝔩 ℌ𝔦𝔤𝔥𝔫𝔢𝔰𝔰 𝔱𝔥𝔢
𝔓𝔯𝔦𝔫𝔠𝔢𝔰𝔰 𝔏𝔬𝔲𝔦𝔰𝔢, 𝔐𝔞𝔯𝔠𝔥𝔦𝔬𝔫𝔢𝔰𝔰 𝔬𝔣 𝔏𝔬𝔯𝔫𝔢.

ARCHÆOLOGICAL SKETCHES
IN
SCOTLAND.

By COLONEL T. P. WHITE,

R. E., F. R. S. EDIN., F. S. A. SCOT.,
OF THE ORDNANCE SURVEY.

VOL. I. KINTYRE.   With 138 Illustrations and a Map.
                   Large folio.
VOL. II. KNAPDALE. With 130 Illustrations and a Map.
                   Large folio.

Price Two Guineas each.

OPINIONS OF THE PRESS.
VOL. I.

"This magnificent volume ought to find a place on the shelves of every lover of Scottish Archæology.......The author has revealed to the general public an invaluable treasure-store of old ecclesiastical traditions, and throws a flood of light on the remote history of Scotland, and its early connection with Ireland.......Discusses in detail every sculptured stone, every old cross, every ruined chapel from north to south; and the engravings are as good, and, as far as we can judge, as faithful as it is possible to have."—*Glasgow Herald.*

"Et Arbejde af stor Betydning for Skandinaviens men særlig for Danmarks og Norges Vedkommende.......Texten er skreven med stor Sagkundskab."—*Copenhagen Fædrelandet.*

Translation.

"A work of great interest for Scandinavians, and specially interesting in the portions relating to Denmark and Norway.......The text is written with great knowledge of the subject."

"Captain White gives the early history of Kintyre from the Irish and Scottish annals, and carefully traces, from their pages, the progress of the original colonisation by men from the north of Ireland their abundant feuds, their battles, and their growth in power...... He deserves the hearty thanks of his readers and the public.......One thing is certain, that he has found many interesting relics.......Many of the relics exhibit a rude approximation to Gothic art; others are still richer and finer, and, in not a few respects, recall the beautiful variety of the early English style."—*Athenæum*.

"The art element forms one of the most interesting features of the volume.......Captain White's volume also affords interesting information respecting various charters and parochial matters. Indeed, we hear that good judges reckon this as one of its strongest points...... The chapters on Saddell Abbey also present much interesting, and, we are inclined to think, novel material.......We may safely pronounce this very handsome volume to be not only a real ornament to the drawing-room table, but also a repertory of a large amount of curious information not easily to be obtained elsewhere in so accessible a shape, and an incentive to the pursuit of archæology, as a study not only connecting us with the past, but important in its bearings upon the present and future of our race."—*Guardian*.

VOL. II.

"On the whole, it is not unfair to describe this volume as a sequel to its forerunner, for the earlier work is an indispensable companion to the later one, especially as regards the historical matter.......Some of the designs on these slabs are extremely beautiful."—*Athenæum*.

"Captain White has practically exhausted the peninsula.......In this volume the author has thoroughly warmed to his work, and drives through it with an intensity that is quite inspiriting.......A series of sketches, often racily written, of scenery and antiquities." —*Scotsman*.

"He" (Captain White) "has done for the sculptured crosses and slabs of Knapdale and Kintyre the same good offices which Mr Stuart did some time ago for the standing-stones of the Eastern counties.......The illustrations made from his own sketches are excellent.......We hope Captain White will continue his work, and erelong give us another volume with drawings as good of the stones of the Isles."—*Saturday Review*.

WILLIAM BLACKWOOD & SONS, EDINBURGH AND LONDON.

CATALOGUE

OF

MESSRS BLACKWOOD & SONS' PUBLICATIONS.

PHILOSOPHICAL CLASSICS FOR ENGLISH READERS.
EDITED BY WILLIAM KNIGHT, LL.D.,
Professor of Moral Philosophy in the University of St Andrews.

In crown 8vo Volumes, with Portraits, price 3s. 6d.

Now ready—

1. **Descartes.** By Professor MAHAFFY, Dublin.
2. **Butler.** By Rev. W. LUCAS COLLINS, M.A.
3. **Berkeley.** By Professor FRASER, Edinburgh.
4. **Fichte.** By Professor ADAMSON, Owens College, Manchester.
5. **Kant.** By Professor WALLACE, Oxford.
6. **Hamilton.** By Professor VEITCH, Glasgow.
7. **Hegel.** By Professor EDWARD CAIRD, Glasgow.
8. **Leibniz.** By J. THEODORE MERZ.
9. **Vico.** By Professor FLINT, Edinburgh.
10. **Hobbes.** By Professor CROOM ROBERTSON, London.

The Volumes in preparation are—

HUME. By the Editor. | SPINOZA. By the Very Rev. Principal Caird, Glasgow.
BACON. By Professor Nichol, Glasgow. |

IN COURSE OF PUBLICATION.

FOREIGN CLASSICS FOR ENGLISH READERS.
EDITED BY MRS OLIPHANT.

In Crown 8vo, 2s. 6d.

The Volumes published are—

DANTE. By the Editor.
VOLTAIRE. By Lieut.-General Sir E. B. Hamley, K.C.B.
PASCAL. By Principal Tulloch.
PETRARCH. By Henry Reeve, C.B.
GOETHE. By A. Hayward, Q C.
MOLIÈRE. By the Editor and F. Tarver, M.A.
MONTAIGNE. By Rev. W. L. Collins, M.A.
RABELAIS. By Walter Besant, M.A.
CALDERON. By E. J. Hasell.

SAINT SIMON. By Clifton W. Collins, M.A.
CERVANTES. By the Editor.
CORNEILLE AND RACINE. By Henry M. Trollope.
MADAME DE SÉVIGNÉ. By Miss Thackeray.
LA FONTAINE, AND OTHER FRENCH FABULISTS. By Rev. W. Lucas Collins, M.A.
SCHILLER. By James Sime, M.A., Author of 'Lessing: his Life and Writings.'
TASSO. By E. J. Hasell.
ROUSSEAU. By Henry Grey Graham.

*In preparation—*LEOPARDI, by the Editor.

NOW COMPLETE.

ANCIENT CLASSICS FOR ENGLISH READERS.
EDITED BY THE REV. W. LUCAS COLLINS, M.A.

Complete in 28 Vols. crown 8vo, cloth, price 2s. 6d. each. And may also be had in 14 Volumes, strongly and neatly bound, with calf or vellum back, £3, 10s.

Saturday Review.—"It is difficult to estimate too highly the value of such a series as this in giving 'English readers' an insight, exact as far as it goes, into those olden times which are so remote and yet to many of us so close."

CATALOGUE

OF

MESSRS BLACKWOOD & SONS'
PUBLICATIONS.

ALISON. History of Europe. By Sir ARCHIBALD ALISON, Bart., D.C.L.
1. From the Commencement of the French Revolution to the Battle of Waterloo.
    LIBRARY EDITION, 14 vols., with Portraits. Demy 8vo, £10, 10s.
    ANOTHER EDITION, in 20 vols. crown 8vo, £6.
    PEOPLE'S EDITION, 13 vols. crown 8vo, £2, 11s.
2. Continuation to the Accession of Louis Napoleon.
    LIBRARY EDITION, 8 vols. 8vo, £6. 7s. 6d.
    PEOPLE'S EDITION, 8 vols. crown 8vo, 34s.
3. Epitome of Alison's History of Europe. Twenty-ninth Thousand. 7s. 6d.
4. Atlas to Alison's History of Europe. By A. Keith Johnston.
    LIBRARY EDITION, demy 4to, £3, 3s.
    PEOPLE'S EDITION, 31s. 6d.

―――― Life of John Duke of Marlborough. With some Account of his Contemporaries, and of the War of the Succession. Third Edition, 2 vols. 8vo. Portraits and Maps. 30s.

―――― Essays: Historical, Political, and Miscellaneous. 3 vols. demy 8vo, 45s.

ADAMS. Great Campaigns. A Succinct Account of the Principal Military Operations which have taken place in Europe from 1796 to 1870. By Major C. ADAMS, Professor of Military History at the Staff College. Edited by Captain C. COOPER KING, R.M. Artillery, Instructor of Tactics, Royal Military College. 8vo, with Maps. 16s.

AIRD. Poetical Works of Thomas Aird. Fifth Edition, with Memoir of the Author by the Rev. JARDINE WALLACE, and Portrait. Crown 8vo, 7s 6d.

ALLARDYCE. The City of Sunshine. By ALEXANDER ALLARDYCE. Three vols. post 8vo, £1, 5s. 6d.

―――― Memoir of the Honourable George Keith Elphinstone, K.B., Viscount Keith of Stonehaven Marischal, Admiral of the Red. One vol. 8vo, with Portrait, Illustrations, and Maps. 21s.

ALMOND. Sermons by a Lay Head-master. By HELY HUTCHINSON ALMOND, M.A. Oxon., Head-master of Loretto School. Crown 8vo, 5s.

ANCIENT CLASSICS FOR ENGLISH READERS. Edited by Rev. W. LUCAS COLLINS, M.A. Complete in 28 vols., cloth, 2s. 6d. each; or in 14 vols., tastefully bound, with calf or vellum back, £3, 10s.

Contents of the Series.

HOMER: THE ILIAD. By the Editor.
HOMER: THE ODYSSEY. By the Editor.
HERODOTUS. By George C. Swayne, M.A.
XENOPHON. By Sir Alexander Grant, Bart., LL.D.
EURIPIDES. By W. B. Donne.
ARISTOPHANES. By the Editor.
PLATO. By Clifton W. Collins, M.A.
LUCIAN. By the Editor.
ÆSCHYLUS. By the Right Rev. the Bishop of Colombo.
SOPHOCLES. By Clifton W. Collins, M.A.
HESIOD AND THEOGNIS. By the Rev. J. Davies, M.A.
GREEK ANTHOLOGY. By Lord Neaves.
VIRGIL. By the Editor.
HORACE. By Sir Theodore Martin, K.C.B.
JUVENAL. By Edward Walford, M.A.
PLAUTUS AND TERENCE. By the Editor.
THE COMMENTARIES OF CÆSAR. By Anthony Trollope.
TACITUS. By W. B. Donne.
CICERO. By the Editor.
PLINY'S LETTERS. By the Rev. Alfred Church, M.A., and the Rev. W. J. Brodribb, M.A.
LIVY. By the Editor.
OVID. By the Rev. A. Church, M.A.
CATULLUS, TIBULLUS, AND PROPERTIUS. By the Rev. Jas. Davies, M.A.
DEMOSTHENES. By the Rev. W. J. Brodribb, M.A.
ARISTOTLE. By Sir Alexander Grant, Bart., LL.D.
THUCYDIDES. By the Editor.
LUCRETIUS. By W. H. Mallock, M.A.
PINDAR. By the Rev. F. D. Morice, M.A.

AYLWARD. The Transvaal of To-day: War, Witchcraft, Sports, and Spoils in South Africa. By ALFRED AYLWARD, Commandant, Transvaal Republic. Second Edition. Crown 8vo, 6s.

AYTOUN. Lays of the Scottish Cavaliers, and other Poems. By W. EDMONDSTOUNE AYTOUN, D.C.L., Professor of Rhetoric and Belles-Lettres in the University of Edinburgh. Thirtieth Edition. Fcap. 8vo, 7s. 6d.

—— Lays of the Scottish Cavaliers, and other Poems. New Edition. 3s. 6d.

—— An Illustrated Edition of the Lays of the Scottish Cavaliers. From designs by Sir NOEL PATON. Small 4to, 21s., in gilt cloth.

—— Bothwell: a Poem. Third Edition. Fcap., 7s. 6d.

—— Firmilian; or, The Student of Badajoz. Fcap., 5s.

—— Poems and Ballads of Goethe. Translated by Professor AYTOUN and Sir THEODORE MARTIN, K.C.B. Third Edition. Fcap., 6s.

—— Bon Gaultier's Book of Ballads. By the SAME. Fourteenth and Cheaper Edition. With Illustrations by Doyle, Leech, and Crowquill. Fcap. 8vo, 5s.

—— The Ballads of Scotland. Edited by Professor AYTOUN. Fourth Edition. 2 vols. fcap. 8vo, 12s.

—— Memoir of William E. Aytoun, D.C.L. By Sir THEODORE MARTIN, K.C.B. With Portrait. Post 8vo, 12s.

BACH. On Musical Education and Vocal Culture. By ALBERT B. BACH. Fourth Edition. 8vo, 7s. 6d.

—— The Principles of Singing. A Practical Guide for Vocalists and Teachers. With Course of Vocal Exercises. Crown 8vo, 6s.

BALLADS AND POEMS. By MEMBERS OF THE GLASGOW BALLAD CLUB. Crown 8vo, 7s. 6d.

BEDFORD. The Regulations of the Old Hospital of the Knights of St John at Valetta. From a Copy Printed at Rome, and preserved in the Archives of Malta; with a Translation, Introduction, and Notes Explanatory of the Hospital Work of the Order. By the Rev. W. K. R. BEDFORD, one of the Chaplains of the Order of St John in England. Royal 8vo, with Frontispiece, Plans, &c., 7s. 6d.

BELLAIRS. The Transvaal War, 1880-81. Edited by Lady BEL-
LAIRS. With a Frontispiece and Map. 8vo, 15s.

BESANT. The Revolt of Man. By WALTER BESANT, M.A.
Seventh Edition. Crown 8vo, 3s. 6d.

—— Readings in Rabelais. Crown 8vo, 7s. 6d.

BEVERIDGE. Culross and Tulliallan; or Perthshire on Forth. Its
History and Antiquities. With Elucidations of Scottish Life and Character
from the Burgh and Kirk-Session Records of that District. By DAVID
BEVERIDGE. 2 vols. 8vo, with Illustrations, 42s.

BLACKIE. Lays and Legends of Ancient Greece. By JOHN
STUART BLACKIE, Emeritus Professor of Greek in the University of Edinburgh. Second Edition. Fcap. 8vo. 5s.

—— The Wisdom of Goethe. Fcap. 8vo. Cloth, extra gilt, 6s.

BLACKWOOD'S MAGAZINE, from Commencement in 1817 to
June 1886. Nos. 1 to 848, forming 138 Volumes.

—— Index to Blackwood's Magazine. Vols. 1 to 50. 8vo, 15s.

—— Tales from Blackwood. Forming Twelve Volumes of
Interesting and Amusing Railway Reading. Price One Shilling each in Paper
Cover. Sold separately at all Railway Bookstalls.
They may also be had bound in cloth, 18s., and in half calf, richly gilt, 30s.
or 12 volumes in 6, Roxburghe, 21s., and half red morocco, 28s.

—— Tales from Blackwood. New Series. Complete in Twenty-
four Shilling Parts. Handsomely bound in 12 vols., cloth, 30s. In leather
back, Roxburghe style, 37s. 6d. In half calf, gilt, 52s. 6d. In half morocco, 55s.

—— Standard Novels. Uniform in size and legibly Printed.
Each Novel complete in one volume.

Florin Series, Illustrated Boards.

TOM CRINGLE'S LOG. By Michael Scott.
THE CRUISE OF THE MIDGE. By the Same.
CYRIL THORNTON. By Captain Hamilton.
ANNALS OF THE PARISH. By John Galt.
THE PROVOST, &c. By John Galt.
SIR ANDREW WYLIE. By John Galt.
THE ENTAIL. By John Galt.
MISS MOLLY. By Beatrice May Butt.
REGINALD DALTON. By J. G. Lockhart.

PEN OWEN. By Dean Hook.
ADAM BLAIR. By J. G. Lockhart.
LADY LEE'S WIDOWHOOD. By General
Sir E. B. Hamley.
SALEM CHAPEL. By Mrs Oliphant.
THE PERPETUAL CURATE. By Mrs Oli-
phant.
MISS MARJORIBANKS. By Mrs Oliphant.
JOHN: A Love Story. By Mrs Oliphant.

Or in Cloth Boards, 2s. 6d.

Shilling Series, Illustrated Cover.

THE RECTOR, and THE DOCTOR'S FAMILY.
By Mrs Oliphant.
THE LIFE OF MANSIE WAUCH. By D. M.
Moir.
PENINSULAR SCENES AND SKETCHES. By
F. Hardman.

SIR FRIZZLE PUMPKIN, NIGHTS AT MESS,
&c.
THE SUBALTERN.
LIFE IN THE FAR WEST. By G. F. Ruxton.
VALERIUS: A Roman Story. By J. G.
Lockhart.

Or in Cloth Boards, 1s. 6d.

BLACKMORE. The Maid of Sker. By R. D. BLACKMORE, Author
of 'Lorna Doone,' &c. Eleventh Edition. Crown 8vo, 7s. 6d.

BOSCOBEL TRACTS. Relating to the Escape of Charles the
Second after the Battle of Worcester, and his subsequent Adventures. Edited
by J. HUGHES, Esq., A.M. A New Edition, with additional Notes and Illustrations, including Communications from the Rev. R. H. BARHAM, Author of
the 'Ingoldsby Legends.' 8vo, with Engravings, 16s.

BROADLEY. Tunis, Past and Present. With a Narrative of the
French Conquest of the Regency. By A. M. BROADLEY. With numerous
Illustrations and Maps. 2 vols. post 8vo. 25s.

BROOKE, Life of Sir James, Rajah of Sarāwak. From his Personal Papers and Correspondence. By SPENSER ST JOHN, H M.'s Minister-Resident and Consul-General Peruvian Republic; formerly Secretary to the Rajah. With Portrait and a Map. Post 8vo, 12s. 6d.

BROUGHAM. Memoirs of the Life and Times of Henry Lord Brougham. Written by HIMSELF. 3 vols. 8vo, £2, 8s. The Volumes are sold separately, price 16s. each.

BROWN. The Forester: A Practical Treatise on the Planting, Rearing, and General Management of Forest-trees By JAMES BROWN, LL.D., Inspector of and Reporter on Woods and Forests, Benmore House, Port Elgin, Ontario. Fifth Edition, revised and enlarged. Royal 8vo, with Engravings. 36s.

BROWN. The Ethics of George Eliot's Works. By JOHN CROMBIE BROWN. Fourth Edition. Crown 8vo, 2s. 6d.

BROWN. A Manual of Botany, Anatomical and Physiological. For the Use of Students. By ROBERT BROWN, M.A., Ph.D. Crown 8vo, with numerous Illustrations, 12s. 6d.

BUCHAN. Introductory Text-Book of Meteorology. By ALEXANDER BUCHAN, M.A., F.R.S.E., Secretary of the Scottish Meteorological Society, &c. Crown 8vo, with 8 Coloured Charts and other Engravings, pp. 218. 4s. 6d.

BUCHANAN. The Shirè Highlands (East Central Africa). By JOHN BUCHANAN, Planter at Zomba. Crown 8vo, 5s.

BURBIDGE. Domestic Floriculture, Window Gardening, and Floral Decorations. Being practical directions for the Propagation, Culture, and Arrangement of Plants and Flowers as Domestic Ornaments. By F. W. BURBIDGE. Second Edition. Crown 8vo, with numerous Illustrations, 7s. 6d.

—— Cultivated Plants: Their Propagation and Improvement. Including Natural and Artificial Hybridisation, Raising from Seed, Cuttings, and Layers, Grafting and Budding, as applied to the Families and Genera in Cultivation. Crown 8vo, with numerous Illustrations, 12s. 6d.

BURTON. The History of Scotland: From Agricola's Invasion to the Extinction of the last Jacobite Insurrection. By JOHN HILL BURTON, D.C.L., Historiographer-Royal for Scotland. New and Enlarged Edition, 8 vols., and Index. Crown 8vo, £3, 3s.

—— History of the British Empire during the Reign of Queen Anne. In 3 vols. 8vo. 36s.

—— The Scot Abroad. Third Edition. Crown 8vo, 10s. 6d.

—— The Book-Hunter. New Edition. Crown 8vo, 7s. 6d.

BUTE. The Roman Breviary: Reformed by Order of the Holy Œcumenical Council of Trent; Published by Order of Pope St Pius V.; and Revised by Clement VIII. and Urban VIII.; together with the Offices since granted. Translated out of Latin into English by JOHN, Marquess of Bute, K.T. In 2 vols. crown 8vo, cloth boards, edges uncut. £2, 2s.

—— The Altus of St Columba. With a Prose Paraphrase and Notes. In paper cover, 2s. 6d.

BUTLER. Pompeii: Descriptive and Picturesque. By W. BUTLER. Post 8vo, 5s.

BUTT. Miss Molly. By BEATRICE MAY BUTT. Cheap Edition, 2s.

—— Alison. 3 vols. crown 8vo, 25s. 6d.

—— Lesterre Durant. 2 vols. crown 8vo. 17s.

CAIRD. Sermons. By JOHN CAIRD, D.D., Principal of the University of Glasgow. Sixteenth Thousand. Fcap. 8vo, 5s.

CAIRD. Religion in Common Life. A Sermon preached in Crathie Church, October 14, 1855, before Her Majesty the Queen and Prince Albert. Published by Her Majesty's Command. By JOHN CAIRD, D.D., Principal of the University of Glasgow. Cheap Edition, 3d.

CAMERON. Gaelic Names of Plants (Scottish and Irish). Collected and Arranged in Scientific Order, with Notes on their Etymology, their Uses, Plant Superstitions, &c., among the Celts, with copious Gaelic, English, and Scientific Indices. By JOHN CAMERON, Sunderland. 8vo, 7s. 6d.

CAMPBELL. Sermons Preached before the Queen at Balmoral. By the Rev. A. A. CAMPBELL, Minister of Crathie. Published by Command of Her Majesty. Crown 8vo, 4s. 6d.

CAMPBELL. Records of Argyll. Legends, Traditions, and Recollections of Argyllshire Highlanders, collected chiefly from the Gaelic. With Notes on the Antiquity of the Dress, Clan Colours or Tartans of the Highlanders. By LORD ARCHIBALD CAMPBELL. Illustrated with Nineteen full-page Etchings. 4to, printed on hand-made paper, £3, 3s.

CAPPON. Victor Hugo. A Memoir and a Study. By JAMES CAPPON, M.A. Post 8vo, 10s 6d.

CARRICK. Koumiss; or, Fermented Mare's Milk: and its Uses in the Treatment and Cure of Pulmonary Consumption, and other Wasting Diseases. With an Appendix on the best Methods of Fermenting Cow's Milk. By GEORGE L. CARRICK, M.D., L.R.C.S.E. and L.R.C.P.E., Physician to the British Embassy, St Petersburg, &c. Crown 8vo, 10s. 6d.

CAUVIN. A Treasury of the English and German Languages. Compiled from the best Authors and Lexicographers in both Languages. Adapted to the Use of Schools, Students, Travellers, and Men of Business; and forming a Companion to all German-English Dictionaries. By JOSEPH CAUVIN, LL.D. & Ph.D., of the University of Göttingen, &c. Crown 8vo, 7s. 6d.

CAVE-BROWN. Lambeth Palace and its Associations. By J. CAVE-BROWN, M.A., Vicar of Detling, Kent, and for many years Curate of Lambeth Parish Church. With an Introduction by the Archbishop of Canterbury. Second Edition, containing an additional Chapter on Medieval Life in the Old Palaces. 8vo, with Illustrations, 21s.

CHARTERIS. Canonicity; or, Early Testimonies to the Existence and Use of the Books of the New Testament. Based on Kirchhoffer's 'Quellensammlung.' Edited by A. H. CHARTERIS, D.D., Professor of Biblical Criticism in the University of Edinburgh. 8vo, 18s.

CHRISTISON. Life of Sir Robert Christison, Bart., M.D., D.C.L. Oxon., Professor of Medical Jurisprudence in the University of Edinburgh. Edited by his SONS. In two vols. 8vo. Vol. I.—Autobiography. 16s. Vol. II.—Memoirs. 16s.

CHURCH SERVICE SOCIETY. A Book on Common Order; Being Forms of Worship issued by the Church Service Society. Fifth Edition, 6s.

CLOUSTON. Popular Tales and Fictions; their Migrations and Transformations. By W. A. CLOUSTON, Editor of 'Arabian Poetry for English Readers,' 'The Book of Sindibad,' &c. 2 vols. post 8vo. [*In the press.*

COCHRAN. A Handy Text-Book of Military Law. Compiled chiefly to assist Officers preparing for Examination; also for all Officers of the Regular and Auxiliary Forces. Specially arranged according to the Syllabus of Subjects of Examination for Promotion, Queen's Regulations, 1883. Comprising also a Synopsis of part of the Army Act. By MAJOR F. COCHRAN, Hampshire Regiment, Garrison Instructor, North British District. Crown 8vo, 7s. 6d.

COLQUHOUN. The Moor and the Loch. Containing Minute Instructions in all Highland Sports, with Wanderings over Crag and Corrie, Flood and Fell. By JOHN COLQUHOUN. Sixth Edition, greatly enlarged. With Illustrations. 2 vols. post 8vo, 26s.

COTTERILL. The Genesis of the Church. By the Right. Rev. HENRY COTTERILL, D.D., Bishop of Edinburgh. Demy 8vo, 16s.

COTTERILL. Suggested Reforms in Public Schools. By C. C. COTTERILL, M.A., Assistant Master at Fettes College, Edin. Crown 8vo, 3s. 6d.

COX. The Opening of the Line: A Strange Story of Dogs and their Doings. By PONSONBY COX. Profusely Illustrated by J. H. O. BROWN. 4to, 3s. 6d.

CRANSTOUN. The Elegies of Albius Tibullus. Translated into English Verse, with Life of the Poet, and Illustrative Notes. By JAMES CRANSTOUN, LL.D., Author of a Translation of 'Catullus.' Crown 8vo, 6s. 6d.

—— The Elegies of Sextus Propertius. Translated into English Verse, with Life of the Poet, and Illustrative Notes. Crown 8vo, 7s. 6d.

CRAWFORD. The Doctrine of Holy Scripture respecting the Atonement. By the late THOMAS J. CRAWFORD, D.D., Professor of Divinity in the University of Edinburgh. Fourth Edition. 8vo, 12s.

—— The Fatherhood of God, Considered in its General and Special Aspects, and particularly in relation to the Atonement, with a Review of Recent Speculations on the Subject. Third Edition, Revised and Enlarged. 8vo, 9s.

—— The Preaching of the Cross, and other Sermons. 8vo, 7s. 6d.

—— The Mysteries of Christianity. Crown 8vo, 7s. 6d.

DAVIES. A Book of Thoughts for every Day in the Year. Selected from the Writings of the Rev. J. LLEWELLYN DAVIES, M.A. By Two CLERGYMEN. Fcap. 8vo, 3s. 6d.

DAVIES. Norfolk Broads and Rivers; or, The Waterways, Lagoons, and Decoys of East Anglia By G. CHRISTOPHER DAVIES, Author of 'The Swan and her Crew.' Illustrated with Seven full-page Plates. New and Cheaper Edition. Crown 8vo, 6s.

DE AINSLIE. Life as I have Found It. By General DE AINSLIE. Post 8vo, 12s. 6d.

DESCARTES. The Method, Meditations, and Principles of Philosophy of Descartes. Translated from the Original French and Latin. With a New Introductory Essay, Historical and Critical, on the Cartesian Philosophy. By JOHN VEITCH, LL.D., Professor of Logic and Rhetoric in the University of Glasgow. A New Edition, being the Eighth. Price 6s. 6d.

DIDON. The Germans. By the Rev. Father DIDON, of the Order of Preaching Friars. Translated into English by RAPHAEL LEDOS DE BEAUFORT. Crown 8vo, 7s. 6d.

DOGS, OUR DOMESTICATED: Their Treatment in reference to Food, Diseases, Habits, Punishment, Accomplishments. By 'MAGENTA.' Crown 8vo, 2s. 6d.

DU CANE. The Odyssey of Homer, Books I.-XII. Translated into English Verse. By Sir CHARLES DU CANE, K.C.M.G. 8vo, 10s. 6d.

DUDGEON. History of the Edinburgh or Queen's Regiment Light Infantry Militia, now 3rd Battalion The Royal Scots; with an Account of the Origin and Progress of the Militia, and a Brief Sketch of the old Royal Scots. By Major R. C. DUDGEON, Adjutant 3rd Battalion The Royal Scots. Post 8vo, with Illustrations, 10s. 6d.

DUNCAN. Manual of the General Acts of Parliament relating to the Salmon Fisheries of Scotland from 1828 to 1882. By J. BARKER DUNCAN. Crown 8vo, 5s.

DUNSMORE. Manual of the Law of Scotland, as to the Relations between Agricultural Tenants and their Landlords, Servants, Merchants, and Bowers. By W. DUNSMORE 8vo, 7s. 6d.

DUPRÉ. Thoughts on Art, and Autobiographical Memoirs of Giovanni Dupré. Translated from the Italian by E. M. PERUZZI, with the permission of the Author. Crown 8vo, 10s. 6d.

ELIOT. George Eliot's Life, Related in her Letters and Journals.
Arranged and Edited by her husband, J. W. CROSS. With Portrait and other
Illustrations. Third Edition. 3 vols. post 8vo, 42s.
—— Works of George Eliot (Cabinet Edition). Handsomely
printed in a new type, 21 volumes, crown 8vo, price £5, 5s. The Volumes
are also sold separately, price 5s. each, viz.:—
Romola. 2 vols.—Silas Marner, The Lifted Veil, Brother Jacob. 1 vol.—
Adam Bede. 2 vols.—Scenes of Clerical Life. 2 vols.—The Mill on
the Floss. 2 vols.—Felix Holt. 2 vols.—Middlemarch. 3 vols.—
Daniel Deronda. 3 vols.—The Spanish Gypsy. 1 vol.—Jubal, and
other Poems, Old and New. 1 vol.—Theophrastus Such. 1 vol.—
Essays. 1 vol.
—— Life of George Eliot. (Cabinet Edition.) With Portrait and
other Illustrations. 3 vols. crown 8vo, 15s.
—— Novels by GEORGE ELIOT. Cheap Edition. Adam Bede. Il-
lustrated. 3s. 6d., cloth.—The Mill on the Floss. Illus-
trated. 3s. 6d., cloth.—Scenes of Clerical Life. Illustrated.
3s., cloth.—Silas Marner: The Weaver of Raveloe. Illus-
trated. 2s. 6d., cloth.—Felix Holt, the Radical. Illustrated.
3s. 6d., cloth.—Romola. With Vignette. 3s. 6d., cloth.
—— Middlemarch. Crown 8vo, 7s. 6d.
—— Daniel Deronda. Crown 8vo, 7s. 6d.
—— Essays. By GEORGE ELIOT. New Edition. Crown 8vo, 5s.
—— Impressions of Theophrastus Such. New Edition. Crown
8vo, 5s.
—— The Spanish Gypsy. Crown 8vo, 5s.
—— The Legend of Jubal, and other Poems, Old and New.
New Edition. Fcap. 8vo, 5s., cloth.
—— Wise, Witty, and Tender Sayings, in Prose and Verse.
Selected from the Works of GEORGE ELIOT. Seventh Edition. Fcap. 8vo, 6s.
—— The George Eliot Birthday Book. Printed on fine paper,
with red border, and handsomely bound in cloth, gilt. Fcap. 8vo, cloth, 3s. 6d.
And in French morocco or Russia, 5s.
ESSAYS ON SOCIAL SUBJECTS. Originally published in
the 'Saturday Review.' A New Edition. First and Second Series. 2 vols.
crown 8vo, 6s. each.
EWALD. The Crown and its Advisers; or, Queen, Ministers,
Lords, and Commons. By ALEXANDER CHARLES EWALD, F.S.A. Crown 8vo,
5s.
FAITHS OF THE WORLD, The. A Concise History of the
Great Religious Systems of the World. By various Authors. Being the St
Giles' Lectures—Second Series. Complete in one volume, crown 8vo, 5s.
FARRER. A Tour in Greece in 1880. By RICHARD RIDLEY
FARRER. With Twenty-seven full-page Illustrations by LORD WINDSOR.
Royal 8vo, with a Map, 21s.
FERRIER. Philosophical Works of the late James F. Ferrier,
B.A. Oxon., Professor of Moral Philosophy and Political Economy, St Andrews.
New Edition. Edited by Sir ALEX. GRANT, Bart., D.C.L., and Professor
LUSHINGTON. 3 vols. crown 8vo, 34s. 6d.
—— Institutes of Metaphysic. Third Edition. 10s. 6d.
—— Lectures on the Early Greek Philosophy. Third Edition,
10s. 6d.
—— Philosophical Remains, including the Lectures on Early
Greek Philosophy. 2 vols., 24s.
FLETCHER. Lectures on the Opening Clauses of the Litany
delivered in St Paul's Church, Edinburgh. By JOHN B. FLETCHER, M.A.
Crown 8vo, 4s.

FLINT. The Philosophy of History in Europe. Vol. I., containing the History of that Philosophy in France and Germany. By ROBERT FLINT, D.D., LL.D., Professor of Divinity, University of Edinburgh. 8vo. *[New Edition in preparation.*

—— Theism. Being the Baird Lecture for 1876. Fifth Edition. Crown 8vo, 7s. 6d.

—— Anti-Theistic Theories. Being the Baird Lecture for 1877. Third Edition Crown 8vo, 10s. 6d.

FORBES. The Campaign of Garibaldi in the Two Sicilies : A Personal Narrative. By CHARLES STUART FORBES, Commander, R.N. Post 8vo, with Portraits, 12s.

FOREIGN CLASSICS FOR ENGLISH READERS. Edited by Mrs OLIPHANT Price 2s. 6d. *For List of Volumes published, see p. 2.*

FRANZOS. The Jews of Barnow. Stories by KARL EMIL FRANZOS. Translated by M. W. MACDOWALL. Crown 8vo, 6s.

GALT. Annals of the Parish. By JOHN GALT. Fcap. 8vo, 2s.

—— The Provost. Fcap. 8vo, 2s.

—— Sir Andrew Wylie. Fcap. 8vo, 2s.

—— The Entail ; or, The Laird of Grippy. Fcap 8vo, 2s.

GENERAL ASSEMBLY OF THE CHURCH OF SCOTLAND.
—— Family Prayers. Authorised by the General Assembly of the Church of Scotland. A New Edition, crown 8vo, in large type, 4s. 6d. Another Edition, crown 8vo, 2s.

—— Prayers for Social and Family Worship. For the Use of Soldiers, Sailors, Colonists, and Sojourners in India, and other Persons, at home and abroad, who are deprived of the ordinary services of a Christian Ministry. Cheap Edition, 1s. 6d.

—— The Scottish Hymnal. Hymns for Public Worship. Published for Use in Churches by Authority of the General Assembly. Various sizes—viz.: 1. Large type, for Pulpit use, cloth, 3s. 6d. 2. Longprimer type, cloth, red edges, 1s. 6d. ; French morocco, 2s. 6d. ; calf, 6s. 3. Bourgeois type, cloth, red edges, 1s. ; French morocco, 2s. 4. Minion type, limp cloth, 6d. ; French morocco, 1s. 6d. 5. School Edition, in paper cover, 2d. 6. Children's Hymnal, paper cover, 1d. No. 2, bound with the Psalms and Paraphrases, cloth, 3s. ; French morocco, 4s. 6d. ; calf, 7s. 6d. No. 3, bound with the Psalms and Paraphrases, cloth, 2s. ; French morocco, 3s.

—— The Scottish Hymnal, with Music. Selected by the Committees on Hymns and on Psalmody The harmonies arranged by W. H. Monk. Cloth, 1s. 6d. ; French morocco, 3s. 6d. The same in the Tonic Sol-fa Notation, 1s. 6d. and 3s. 6d.

—— The Scottish Hymnal, with Fixed Tune for each Hymn. Longprimer type, 3s. 6d.

—— The Scottish Hymnal Appendix. 1. Longprimer type, 1s. 2. Nonpareil type, cloth limp, 4d ; paper cover, 2d

—— Scottish Hymnal with Appendix Incorporated. Bourgeois type, limp cloth, 1s. Large type, cloth, red edges, 2s. 6d. Nonpareil type, paper covers, 3d. ; cloth, red edges, 6d.

GERARD. Reata : What's in a Name. By E. D. GERARD. New Edition. Crown 8vo, 6s.

—— Beggar my Neighbour. New Edition. Crown 8vo, 6s.

—— The Waters of Hercules. New Edition. Crown 8vo, 6s.

GOETHE'S FAUST. Part I. Translated into English Verse by Sir THEODORE MARTIN, K.C.B. Second Edition, post 8vo, 6s. Eighth Edition, fcap., 3s. 6d.

GOETHE'S FAUST. Part II. Translated into English Verse by Sir THEODORE MARTIN, K.C.B. Fcap 8vo, 6s.

GOETHE. Poems and Ballads of Goethe. Translated by Professor AYTOUN and Sir THEODORE MARTIN, K.C.B. Third Edition, fcap. 8vo, 6s.

GORDON CUMMING. At Home in Fiji. By C. F. GORDON CUMMING, Author of 'From the Hebrides to the Himalayas.' Fourth Edition, post 8vo. With Illustrations and Map. 7s. 6d.

—— A Lady's Cruise in a French Man-of-War. New and Cheaper Edition. 8vo. With Illustrations and Map. 12s. 6d.

—— Fire-Fountains. The Kingdom of Hawaii : Its Volcanoes, and the History of its Missions. With Map and numerous Illustrations. 2 vols. 8vo, 25s.

—— Granite Crags: The Yō-semité Region of California. With Illustrations. New Edition. Post 8vo, 8s. 6d.

—— Wanderings in China. Second Edition. 2 vols. 8vo, with Illustrations, 25s.

GRAHAM. The Life and Work of Syed Ahmed Khan, C.S.I. By Lieut.-Colonel G. F I. GRAHAM, B.S.C. 8vo, 14s.

GRANT. Bush-Life in Queensland. By A. C. GRANT. New Edition, Crown 8vo, 6s.

HALDANE. Subtropical Cultivation and Climates. A Handy Book for Planters, Colonists, and Settlers. By R. C. HALDANE. Post 8vo, 9s.

HAMERTON. Wenderholme : A Story of Lancashire and Yorkshire Life. By PHILIP GILBERT HAMERTON, Author of 'A Painter's Camp.' A New Edition. Crown 8vo, 6s.

HAMILTON. Lectures on Metaphysics. By Sir WILLIAM HAMILTON, Bart., Professor of Logic and Metaphysics in the University of Edinburgh. Edited by the Rev. H. L. MANSEL, B.D., LL.D., Dean of St Paul's ; and JOHN VEITCH, M.A., Professor of Logic and Rhetoric, Glasgow. Seventh Edition. 2 vols. 8vo, 24s.

—— Lectures on Logic. Edited by the SAME. Third Edition. 2 vols., 24s.

—— Discussions on Philosophy and Literature, Education and University Reform. Third Edition, 8vo, 21s.

—— Memoir of Sir William Hamilton, Bart., Professor of Logic and Metaphysics in the University of Edinburgh. By Professor VEITCH of the University of Glasgow. 8vo, with Portrait, 18s.

—— Sir William Hamilton: The Man and his Philosophy. Two Lectures Delivered before the Edinburgh Philosophical Institution, January and February 1883. By the SAME. Crown 8vo, 2s.

HAMLEY. The Operations of War Explained and Illustrated. By Lieut.-General Sir EDWARD BRUCE HAMLEY, K.C.B. Fourth Edition, revised throughout. 4to, with numerous Illustrations, 30s.

—— Thomas Carlyle : An Essay. Second Edition. Crown 8vo. 2s. 6d.

—— The Story of the Campaign of Sebastopol. Written in the Camp. With Illustrations drawn in Camp by the Author. 8vo, 21s.

—— On Outposts. Second Edition. 8vo, 2s.

—— Wellington's Career ; A Military and Political Summary. Crown 8vo, 2s.

—— Lady Lee's Widowhood. Crown 8vo, 2s. 6d.

—— Our Poor Relations. A Philozoic Essay. With Illustrations, chiefly by Ernest Griset. Crown 8vo, cloth gilt, 3s. 6d.

HAMLEY. Guilty, or Not Guilty ? A Tale. By Major-General W. G. HAMLEY, late of the Royal Engineers. New Edition. Crown 8vo, 3s. 6d.

—— Traseaden Hall. "When George the Third was King." New and Cheaper Edition. Crown 8vo, 6s.

HARBORD. Definitions and Diagrams in Astronomy and Navigation. By the Rev. J. B. HARBORD, M.A., Assistant Director of Education, Admiralty. 1s.

——— Short Sermons for Hospitals and Sick Seamen. Fcap. 8vo, cloth, 4s. 6d.

HARRISON. Oure Tounis Colledge. Sketches of the History of the Old College of Edinburgh, with an Appendix of Historical Documents. By JOHN HARRISON. Crown 8vo, 5s.

HASELL. Bible Partings. By E. J. HASELL. Crown 8vo, 6s.

——— Short Family Prayers. By Miss HASELL. Cloth, 1s.

HAY. The Works of the Right Rev. Dr George Hay, Bishop of Edinburgh. Edited under the Supervision of the Right Rev. Bishop STRAIN. With Memoir and Portrait of the Author. 5 vols. crown 8vo, bound in extra cloth, £1, 1s. Or, sold separately—viz.:

The Sincere Christian Instructed in the Faith of Christ from the Written Word. 2 vols., 8s.—The Devout Christian Instructed in the Law of Christ from the Written Word. 2 vols., 8s.—The Pious Christian Instructed in the Nature and Practice of the Principal Exercises of Piety. 1 vol., 4s.

HEATLEY. The Horse-Owner's Safeguard. A Handy Medical Guide for every Man who owns a Horse. By G. S. HEATLEY, M.R.C., V.S. Crown 8vo, 5s.

——— The Stock-Owner's Guide. A Handy Medical Treatise for every Man who owns an Ox or a Cow. Crown 8vo, 4s. 6d.

HEMANS. The Poetical Works of Mrs Hemans. Copyright Editions.—One Volume, royal 8vo, 5s.—The Same, with Illustrations engraved on Steel, bound in cloth, gilt edges, 7s. 6d.—Six Volumes in Three, fcap., 12s. 6d. SELECT POEMS OF MRS HEMANS. Fcap., cloth, gilt edges, 3s.

HOLE. A Book about Roses: How to Grow and Show Them. By the Rev. Canon HOLE. Ninth Edition, revised. Crown 8vo, 3s. 6d.

HOME PRAYERS. By Ministers of the Church of Scotland and Members of the Church Service Society. Second Edition. Fcap. 8vo, 3s.

HOMER. The Odyssey. Translated into English Verse in the Spenserian Stanza. By PHILIP STANHOPE WORSLEY. Third Edition, 2 vols. fcap., 12s.

——— The Iliad. Translated by P. S. WORSLEY and Professor CONINGTON. 2 vols. crown 8vo, 21s.

HOSACK. Mary Queen of Scots and Her Accusers. Containing a Variety of Documents never before published. By JOHN HOSACK, Barrister-at-Law. A New and Enlarged Edition, with a Photograph from the Bust on the Tomb in Westminster Abbey. 2 vols. 8vo, £1, 1s.

HUTCHINSON. Hints on the Game of Golf. By HORACE G. HUTCHINSON. Fcap. 8vo, 1s. 6d.

HYDE. The Royal Mail; its Curiosities and Romance. By JAMES WILSON HYDE, Superintendent in the General Post Office, Edinburgh. Second Edition, enlarged. Crown 8vo, with Illustrations, 6s.

INDEX GEOGRAPHICUS: Being a List, alphabetically arranged, of the Principal Places on the Globe, with the Countries and Subdivisions of the Countries in which they are situated, and their Latitudes and Longitudes. Applicable to all Modern Atlases and Maps. Imperial 8vo, pp. 676, 21s.

JEAN JAMBON. Our Trip to Blunderland; or, Grand Excursion to Blundertown and Back. By JEAN JAMBON. With Sixty Illustrations designed by CHARLES DOYLE, engraved by DALZIEL. Fourth Thousand. Handsomely bound in cloth, gilt edges, 6s. 6d. Cheap Edition, cloth, 3s. 6d. In boards, 2s. 6d.

JERNINGHAM. Reminiscences of an Attaché. By HUBERT E. H. JERNINGHAM. Second Edition. Crown 8vo, 5s.

JOHNSON. The Scots Musical Museum. Consisting of upwards of Six Hundred Songs, with proper Basses for the Pianoforte. Originally published by JAMES JOHNSON; and now accompanied with Copious Notes and Illustrations of the Lyric Poetry and Music of Scotland, by the late WILLIAM STENHOUSE; with additional Notes and Illustrations, by DAVID LAING and C. K. SHARPE. 4 vols. 8vo, Roxburghe binding.

JOHNSTON. The Chemistry of Common Life. By Professor J. F. W. JOHNSTON. New Edition, Revised, and brought down to date. By ARTHUR HERBERT CHURCH, M.A. OXON.; Author of 'Food: its Sources, Constituents, and Uses;' 'The Laboratory Guide for Agricultural Students;' 'Plain Words about Water,' &c. Illustrated with Maps and 102 Engravings on Wood. Complete in one volume, crown 8vo, pp. 618, 7s. 6d.

—— Elements of Agricultural Chemistry and Geology. Thirteenth Edition. Revised, and brought down to date. By Sir CHARLES A. CAMERON, M.D., F.R.C.S.I., &c. Fcap. 8vo, 6s. 6d.

—— Catechism of Agricultural Chemistry and Geology. An entirely New Edition, revised and enlarged, by Sir CHARLES A. CAMERON, M.D., F.R.C.S.I., &c. Eighty-sixth Thousand, with numerous Illustrations, 1s.

JOHNSTON. Patrick Hamilton: a Tragedy of the Reformation in Scotland, 1528. By T. P. JOHNSTON. Crown 8vo, with Two Etchings by the Author, 5s.

KENNEDY. Sport, Travel, and Adventures in Newfoundland and the West Indies. By Captain W. R. KENNEDY, R.N. With Illustrations by the Author. Post 8vo, 14s.

KING. The Metamorphoses of Ovid. Translated in English Blank Verse. By HENRY KING, M.A., Fellow of Wadham College, Oxford, and of the Inner Temple, Barrister-at-Law. Crown 8vo, 10s. 6d.

KINGLAKE. History of the Invasion of the Crimea. By A. W. KINGLAKE. Cabinet Edition. Seven Volumes, illustrated with maps and plans, crown 8vo, at 6s. each. The Volumes respectively contain:—
I. THE ORIGIN OF THE WAR between the Czar and the Sultan. II. RUSSIA MET AND INVADED. III. THE BATTLE OF THE ALMA. IV. SEBASTOPOL AT BAY. V. THE BATTLE OF BALACLAVA. VI. THE BATTLE OF INKERMAN. VII. WINTER TROUBLES.

—— History of the Invasion of the Crimea. Vol. VI. Winter Troubles. Demy 8vo, with a Map, 16s.

—— History of the Invasion of the Crimea. Vol. VII. Demy 8vo. [In preparation.

—— Eothen. A New Edition, uniform with the Cabinet Edition of the 'History of the Crimean War,' price 6s.

KNOLLYS. The Elements of Field-Artillery. Designed for the Use of Infantry and Cavalry Officers. By HENRY KNOLLYS, Captain Royal Artillery; Author of 'From Sedan to Saarbrück,' Editor of 'Incidents in the Sepoy War,' &c. With Engravings. Crown 8vo, 7s. 6d.

LAING. Select Remains of the Ancient Popular and Romance Poetry of Scotland. Originally Collected and Edited by DAVID LAING, LL.D. Re-edited, with Memorial-Introduction, by JOHN SMALL, M.A. With a Portrait of Dr Laing. 4to, 25s.

LAVERGNE. The Rural Economy of England, Scotland, and Ireland. By LEONCE DE LAVERGNE. Translated from the French. With Notes by a Scottish Farmer. 8vo, 12s.

LAWLESS. Hurrish: a Study. By the Hon. EMILY LAWLESS, Author of 'A Chelsea Householder,' 'A Millionaire's Cousin.' Second Edition, crown 8vo, 6s.

LEE. Miss Brown: A Novel. By VERNON LEE. 3 vols. post 8vo, 25s. 6d.

LEE. Glimpses in the Twilight. Being various Notes, Records, and Examples of the Supernatural. By the Rev. GEORGE F. LEE, D.C.L. Crown 8vo. 8s. 6d.

LEE-HAMILTON. Poems and Transcripts. By EUGENE LEE-HAMILTON. Crown 8vo, 6s.

LEES. A Handbook of Sheriff Court Styles. By J. M. LEES, M.A., LL.B., Advocate, Sheriff-Substitute of Lanarkshire. 8vo, 16s.

——— A Handbook of the Sheriff and Justice of Peace Small Debt Courts. 8vo, 7s. 6d.

LETTERS FROM THE HIGHLANDS. Reprinted from 'The Times.' Fcap. 8vo, 4s. 6d.

LINDAU. The Philosopher's Pendulum and other Stories. By RUDOLPH LINDAU. Crown 8vo, 7s. 6d.

LITTLE. Madagascar: Its History and People. By the Rev. HENRY W. LITTLE, some years Missionary in East Madagascar. Post 8vo, 10s. 6d.

LOCKHART. Doubles and Quits. By LAURENCE W. M. LOCKHART. With Twelve Illustrations. Fourth Edition. Crown 8vo, 6s.

——— Fair to See: a Novel. Eighth Edition. Crown 8vo, 6s.

——— Mine is Thine: a Novel. Eighth Edition. Crown 8vo, 6s.

LORIMER. The Institutes of Law: A Treatise of the Principles of Jurisprudence as determined by Nature. By JAMES LORIMER, Regius Professor of Public Law and of the Law of Nature and Nations in the University of Edinburgh. New Edition, revised throughout, and much enlarged. 8vo, 18s.

——— The Institutes of the Law of Nations. A Treatise of the Jural Relation of Separate Political Communities. In 2 vols. 8vo. Volume I., price 16s. Volume II., price 20s.

M'COMBIE. Cattle and Cattle-Breeders. By WILLIAM M'COMBIE, Tillyfour. New Edition, enlarged, and with Memoir of the Author. By JAMES MACDONALD, Editor of the 'Live-Stock Journal.' 3s. 6d.

MACRAE. A Handbook of Deer-Stalking. By ALEXANDER MACRAE, late Forester to Lord Henry Bentinck. With Introduction by HORATIO ROSS, Esq. Fcap 8vo, with two Photographs from Life. 3s. 6d.

M'CRIE. Works of the Rev. Thomas M'Crie, D.D. Uniform Edition. Four vols. crown 8vo, 24s.

——— Life of John Knox. Containing Illustrations of the History of the Reformation in Scotland. Crown 8vo, 6s. Another Edition, 3s. 6d.

——— Life of Andrew Melville. Containing Illustrations of the Ecclesiastical and Literary History of Scotland in the Sixteenth and Seventeenth Centuries. Crown 8vo, 6s.

——— History of the Progress and Suppression of the Reformation in Italy in the Sixteenth Century. Crown 8vo, 4s.

——— History of the Progress and Suppression of the Reformation in Spain in the Sixteenth Century. Crown 8vo, 3s. 6d.

——— Lectures on the Book of Esther. Fcap. 8vo, 5s.

M'INTOSH. The Book of the Garden. By CHARLES M'INTOSH, formerly Curator of the Royal Gardens of his Majesty the King of the Belgians, and lately of those of his Grace the Duke of Buccleuch, K.G., at Dalkeith Palace. Two large vols. royal 8vo, embellished with 1350 Engravings. £4, 7s. 6d. Vol. I. On the Formation of Gardens and Construction of Garden Edifices. 776 pages, and 1073 Engravings, £2, 10s.

Vol. II. Practical Gardening. 868 pages, and 279 Engravings, £1, 17s. 6d.

MACKAY. A Manual of Modern Geography; Mathematical, Physical, and Political. By the Rev. ALEXANDER MACKAY, LL.D., F.R.G.S. 11th Edition, revised to the present time. Crown 8vo, pp. 688. 7s. 6d.
—— Elements of Modern Geography. 51st Thousand, revised to the present time. Crown 8vo, pp 300. 3s.
—— The Intermediate Geography. Intended as an Intermediate Book between the Author's 'Outlines of Geography' and 'Elements of Geography.' Eleventh Edition, revised Crown 8vo, pp. 238. 2s.
—— Outlines of Modern Geography. 175th Thousand, revised to the present time. 18mo, pp. 118. 1s.
—— First Steps in Geography. 82d Thousand. 18mo, pp. 56. Sewed, 4d.; cloth, 6d
—— Elements of Physiography and Physical Geography. With Express Reference to the Instructions recently issued by the Science and Art Department. 25th Thousand, revised. Crown 8vo, 1s. 6d.
—— Facts and Dates; or, the Leading Events in Sacred and Profane History, and the Principal Facts in the various Physical Sciences. The Memory being aided throughout by a Simple and Natural Method. For Schools and Private Reference. New Edition Crown 8vo, 3s. 6d.
MACKAY. An Old Scots Brigade. Being the History of Mackay's Regiment, now incorporated with the Royal Scots. With an Appendix containing many Original Documents connected with the History of the Regiment. By JOHN MACKAY (late) of HERRIESDALE. Crown 8vo, 5s.
MACKAY. The Founders of the American Republic. A History of Washington, Adams, Jefferson, Franklin, and Madison. With a Supplementary Chapter on the Inherent Causes of the Ultimate Failure of American Democracy. By CHARLES MACKAY, LL.D Post 8vo, 10s. 6d.
MACKELLAR. More Leaves from the Journal of a Life in the Highlands, from 1862 to 1882. Translated into Gaelic by Mrs MARY MACKELLAR. By command of Her Majesty the Queen. Crown 8vo, with Illustrations. 10s. 6d.
MACKENZIE. Studies in Roman Law. With Comparative Views of the Laws of France, England, and Scotland By LORD MACKENZIE, one of the Judges of the Court of Session in Scotland. Fifth Edition, Edited by JOHN KIRKPATRICK, Esq., M.A. Cantab.; Dr Jur. Heidelb.; LL.B., Edin.; Advocate. 8vo, 12s.
MADOC. Thereby. A Novel. By FAYR MADOC. Two vols. Post 8vo, 17s.
MAIN. Three Hundred English Sonnets. Chosen and Edited by DAVID M. MAIN. Fcap. 8vo, 6s.
MANNERS. Notes of an Irish Tour in 1846. By Lord JOHN MANNERS, M.P., G.C.B. New Edition Crown 8vo, 2s 6d.
MANNERS. Gems of German Poetry. Translated by Lady JOHN MANNERS. Small quarto, 3s. 6d
—— Impressions of Bad-Homburg. Comprising a Short Account of the Women's Associations of Germany under the Red Cross. By Lady JOHN MANNERS. Crown 8vo, 1s. 6d.
—— Some Personal Recollections of the Later Years of the Earl of Beaconsfield, K.G. Sixth Edition, 6d.
—— Employment of Women in the Public Service. 6d.
—— Some of the Advantages of Easily Accessible Reading and Recreation Rooms, and Free Libraries. With Remarks on Starting and Maintaining Them Second Edition, crown 8vo, 1s.
—— Encouraging Experiences of Reading and Recreation Rooms. Crown 8vo, 1s.
—— A Sequel to Rich Men's Dwellings, and other Occasional Papers. Crown 8vo, 2s. 6d.
MARMORNE. The Story is told by ADOLPHUS SEGRAVE, the youngest of three Brothers. Third Edition. Crown 8vo, 6s.

MARSHALL. French Home Life. By FREDERIC MARSHALL. Second Edition. 5s.

MARSHMAN. History of India. From the Earliest Period to the Close of the India Company's Government; with an Epitome of Subsequent Events. By JOHN CLARK MARSHMAN, C.S.I. Abridged from the Author's larger work. Second Edition, revised. Crown 8vo, with Map, 6s. 6d.

MARTIN. Goethe's Faust. Part I. Translated by Sir THEODORE MARTIN, K C.B. Second Edition, crown 8vo, 6s. Eighth Edition, 3s. 6d.

——— Goethe's Faust. Part II. Translated into English Verse. Second Edition, revised. Fcap. 8vo, 6s.

——— The Works of Horace. Translated into English Verse, with Life and Notes. In 2 vols. crown 8vo, printed on hand-made paper, 21s.

——— Poems and Ballads of Heinrich Heine. Done into English Verse. Second Edition. Printed on papier vergé, crown 8vo, 8s.

——— Catullus. With Life and Notes. Second Edition, post 8vo, 7s. 6d.

——— The Vita Nuova of Dante. With an Introduction and Notes. Second Edition, crown 8vo, 5s.

——— Aladdin: A Dramatic Poem. By ADAM OEHLENSCHLAEGER. Fcap. 8vo, 5s.

——— Correggio: A Tragedy. By OEHLENSCHLAEGER. With Notes. Fcap. 8vo, 3s.

——— King Rene's Daughter: A Danish Lyrical Drama. By HENRIK HERTZ. Second Edition, fcap., 2s. 6d.

MARTIN. Some of Shakespeare's Female Characters. In a Series of Letters. By HELENA FAUCIT, LADY MARTIN. With Portraits engraved by the late F. Holl. Dedicated by Special Permission to Her Most Gracious Majesty the Queen. 4to. printed on hand-made paper.

MATHESON. Can the Old Faith Live with the New? or the Problem of Evolution and Revelation. By the Rev. GEORGE MATHESON, D.D. Second Edition. Crown 8vo, 7s. 6d.

MEIKLEJOHN. An Old Educational Reformer—Dr Bell. By J. M. D. MEIKLEJOHN, M.A., Professor of the Theory, History, and Practice of Education in the University of St Andrews. Crown 8vo, 3s. 6d.

——— The Golden Primer. With Coloured Illustrations by Walter Crane. Small 4to, boards, 5s.

——— The English Language: Its Grammar, History, and Literature. With Chapters on Composition, Versification, Pharaphrasing, and Punctuation. Crown 8vo, 4s. 6d.

MICHEL. A Critical Inquiry into the Scottish Language. With the view of Illustrating the Rise and Progress of Civilisation in Scotland. By FRANCISQUE-MICHEL, F.S.A. Lond. and Scot., Correspondant de l'Institut de France, &c. In One handsome Quarto Volume, printed on hand-made paper, and appropriately bound in Roxburghe style. Price 66s.

MICHIE. The Larch: Being a Practical Treatise on its Culture and General Management. By CHRISTOPHER Y. MICHIE, Forester, Cullen House. Crown 8vo, with Illustrations. New and Cheaper Edition, enlarged, 5s.

MILLIONAIRE, THE. By LOUIS J. JENNINGS, Author of 'Field Paths and Green Lanes,' 'Rambles among the Hills,' &c. Second Edition. 2 vols. crown 8vo, 25s. 6d.

MILNE. The Problem of the Churchless and Poor in our Large Towns. With special reference to the Home Mission Work of the Church of Scotland. By the Rev. ROBT. MILNE, M.A., Towie. Crown 8vo, 5s.

MINTO. A Manual of English Prose Literature, Biographical and Critical: designed mainly to show Characteristics of Style. By W. MINTO, M.A., Professor of Logic in the University of Aberdeen. New Edition, revised. Crown 8vo, 7s. 6d.

——— Characteristics of English Poets, from Chaucer to Shirley. New Edition, revised. Crown 8vo, 7s. 6d.

MINTO. The Crack of Doom. Originally published in 'Blackwood's Magazine.' 3 vols. post 8vo, 25s. 6d.

MITCHELL. Biographies of Eminent Soldiers of the last Four Centuries. By Major-General JOHN MITCHELL, Author of 'Life of Wallenstein.' With a Memoir of the Author. 8vo, 9s.

MOIR. Life of Mansie Wauch, Tailor in Dalkeith. With 8 Illustrations on Steel, by the late GEORGE CRUIKSHANK. Crown 8vo, 3s. 6d. Another Edition, fcap. 8vo, 1s. 6d.

MOMERIE. Defects of Modern Christianity, and other Sermons. By the Rev. A. W. MOMERIE, M.A., D.Sc., Professor of Logic and Metaphysics in King's College, London. New Edition. Crown 8vo, 5s.

—— The Basis of Religion. Being an Examination of Natural Religion. Second Edition. Crown 8vo, 2s. 6d.

—— The Origin of Evil, and other Sermons. Fourth Edition, enlarged. Crown 8vo, 5s.

—— Personality. The Beginning and End of Metaphysics, and a Necessary Assumption in all Positive Philosophy. Third Edition. Crown 8vo, 3s.

—— Agnosticism, and other Sermons. Crown 8vo, 6s.

MONTAGUE. Campaigning in South Africa. Reminiscences of an Officer in 1879. By Captain W. E. MONTAGUE, 94th Regiment, Author of 'Claude Meadowleigh,' &c. 8vo, 10s. 6d.

MONTALEMBERT. Memoir of Count de Montalembert. A Chapter of Recent French History. By Mrs OLIPHANT, Author of the 'Life of Edward Irving,' &c. 2 vols. crown 8vo, £1, 4s.

MURDOCH. Manual of the Law of Insolvency and Bankruptcy: Comprehending a Summary of the Law of Insolvency, Notour Bankruptcy, Composition-contracts, Trust-deeds, Cessios, and Sequestrations; and the Winding-up of Joint-Stock Companies in Scotland; with Annotations on the various Insolvency and Bankruptcy Statutes; and with Forms of Procedure applicable to these Subjects. By JAMES MURDOCH, Member of the Faculty of Procurators in Glasgow. Fifth Edition, Revised and Enlarged, 8vo, £1, 10s.

MY TRIVIAL LIFE AND MISFORTUNE: A Gossip with no Plot in Particular. By A PLAIN WOMAN. New Edition, crown 8vo, 6s.

NASEBY. Oaks and Birches. A Novel. By NASEBY. 3 vols. crown 8vo, 25s. 6d.

NEAVES. Songs and Verses, Social and Scientific. By an Old Contributor to 'Maga.' By the Hon. Lord NEAVES. Fifth Edition, fcap. 8vo, 4s.

—— The Greek Anthology. Being Vol. XX. of 'Ancient Classics for English Readers.' Crown 8vo, 2s. 6d.

NICHOLSON. A Manual of Zoology, for the Use of Students. With a General Introduction on the Principles of Zoology. By HENRY ALLEYNE NICHOLSON, M.D., D.Sc., F.L.S., F.G.S., Regius Professor of Natural History in the University of Aberdeen. Sixth Edition, revised and enlarged. Crown 8vo, pp. 865, with 454 Engravings on Wood, 14s.

—— Text-Book of Zoology, for the Use of Schools. Fourth Edition, enlarged. Crown 8vo, with 188 Engravings on Wood, 7s. 6d.

—— Introductory Text-Book of Zoology, for the Use of Junior Classes. Fifth Edition, revised and enlarged, with 166 Engravings, 3s.

—— Outlines of Natural History, for Beginners; being Descriptions of a Progressive Series of Zoological Types. Third Edition, with Engravings, 1s. 6d.

—— A Manual of Palæontology, for the Use of Students. With a General Introduction on the Principles of Palæontology. Second Edition. Revised and greatly enlarged. 2 vols. 8vo, with 722 Engravings, £2, 2s.

—— The Ancient Life-History of the Earth. An Outline of the Principles and Leading Facts of Palæontological Science. Crown 8vo, with 276 Engravings, 10s. 6d.

NICHOLSON. On the "Tabulate Corals" of the Palæozoic Period, with Critical Descriptions of Illustrative Species. By HENRY ALLEYNE NICHOLSON, M.D., D.Sc., F.L.S., F.G.S., Regius Professor of Natural History in the University of Aberdeen. Illustrated with 15 Lithograph Plates and numerous Engravings. Super-royal 8vo, 21s.

—— On the Structure and Affinities of the Genus Monticulipora and its Sub-Genera, with Critical Descriptions of Illustrative Species. Illustrated with numerous Engravings on wood and lithographed Plates. Super-royal 8vo, 18s.

—— Synopsis of the Classification of the Animal Kingdom. 8vo, with 106 Illustrations, 6s.

NICHOLSON. Communion with Heaven, and other Sermons. By the late MAXWELL NICHOLSON, D.D., Minister of St Stephen's, Edinburgh. Crown 8vo, 5s. 6d.

—— Rest in Jesus. Sixth Edition. Fcap. 8vo, 4s. 6d.

OLIPHANT. Masollam: a Problem of the Period. A Novel. By LAURENCE OLIPHANT. 3 vols. post 8vo, 25s. 6d.

—— Altiora Peto. Eighth Edition, Illustrated. Crown 8vo, 6s.

—— Piccadilly: A Fragment of Contemporary Biography. With Eight Illustrations by Richard Doyle. Eighth Edition, 4s. 6d. Cheap Edition, in paper cover, 2s. 6d.

—— Traits and Travesties; Social and Political. Post 8vo, 10s. 6d.

—— The Land of Gilead. With Excursions in the Lebanon. With Illustrations and Maps. Demy 8vo, 21s.

—— The Land of Khemi. Post 8vo, with Illustrations, 10s. 6d.

—— Haifa: Life in Modern Palestine. With numerous Illustrations and Diagrams. 1 vol. 8vo. [In preparation.

—— Sympneumata: or, Evolutionary Functions now Active in Man. Edited by LAURENCE OLIPHANT. Post 8vo, 10s. 6d.

OLIPHANT. The Story of Valentine; and his Brother. By Mrs OLIPHANT. 5s., cloth.

—— Katie Stewart. 2s. 6d.

—— A House Divided against Itself. 3 vols. post 8vo, 25s. 6d.

OSBORN. Narratives of Voyage and Adventure. By Admiral SHERARD OSBORN, C.B. 3 vols. crown 8vo, 12s.

OSSIAN. The Poems of Ossian in the Original Gaelic. With a Literal Translation into English, and a Dissertation on the Authenticity of the Poems. By the Rev. ARCHIBALD CLERK. 2 vols. imperial 8vo, £1, 11s. 6d.

OSWALD. By Fell and Fjord; or, Scenes and Studies in Iceland. By E. J. OSWALD. Post 8vo, with Illustrations. 7s. 6d.

OUTRAM. Lyrics: Legal and Miscellaneous. By the late GEORGE OUTRAM, Esq., Advocate. New Edition, Revised. With Illustrations.
[In the press.

PAGE. Introductory Text-Book of Geology. By DAVID PAGE, LL.D., Professor of Geology in the Durham University of Physical Science, Newcastle. With Engravings on Wood and Glossarial Index. Eleventh Edition, 2s. 6d.

—— Advanced Text-Book of Geology, Descriptive and Industrial. With Engravings, and Glossary of Scientific Terms. Sixth Edition, revised and enlarged, 7s. 6d.

—— Introductory Text-Book of Physical Geography. With Sketch-Maps and Illustrations. Edited by CHARLES LAPWORTH, F.G.S., &c., Professor of Geology and Mineralogy in the Mason Science College, Birmingham. 11th Edition. 2s. 6d.

—— Advanced Text-Book of Physical Geography. Third Edition, Revised and Enlarged by Professor LAPWORTH. With Engravings. 5s.

WILLIAM BLACKWOOD AND SONS. 19

PATON. Spindrift. By Sir J. NOEL PATON. Fcap., cloth, 5s.
—— Poems by a Painter. Fcap., cloth, 5s.
PATTERSON. Essays in History and Art. By R. HOGARTH PATTERSON. 8vo, 12s.
—— The New Golden Age, and Influence of the Precious Metals upon the World. 2 vols. 8vo, 31s. 6d.
PAUL. History of the Royal Company of Archers, the Queen's Body-Guard for Scotland. By JAMES BALFOUR PAUL, Advocate of the Scottish Bar. Crown 4to, with Portraits and other Illustrations. £2, 2s.
PAUL. Analysis and Critical Interpretation of the Hebrew Text of the Book of Genesis. Preceded by a Hebrew Grammar, and Dissertations on the Genuineness of the Pentateuch, and on the Structure of the Hebrew Language. By the Rev. WILLIAM PAUL, A.M. 8vo, 18s.
PETTIGREW. The Handy Book of Bees, and their Profitable Management. By A. PETTIGREW. Fourth Edition, Enlarged, with Engravings. Crown 8vo, 3s. 6d.
PHILOSOPHICAL CLASSICS FOR ENGLISH READERS. Companion Series to Ancient and Foreign Classics for English Readers. Edited by WILLIAM KNIGHT, LL.D., Professor of Moral Philosophy, University of St Andrews. In crown 8vo volumes, with portraits, price 3s. 6d.

1. DESCARTES. By Professor Mahaffy, Dublin.
2. BUTLER. By the Rev. W. Lucas Collins, M.A.
3. BERKELEY. By Professor A. Campbell Fraser, Edinburgh.
4. FICHTE. By Professor Adamson, Manchester.
5. KANT. By Professor Wallace, Oxford.
6. HAMILTON. By Professor Veitch, Glasgow.
7. HEGEL. By Professor Edward Caird, Glasgow.
8. LEIBNIZ. By J. Theodore Merz.
9. VICO. By Professor Flint, Edinburgh.
10. HOBBES. By Professor Croom Robertson, London.
11. HUME. By the Editor. [Shortly.

POLLOK. The Course of Time: A Poem. By ROBERT POLLOK, A.M. Small fcap. 8vo, cloth gilt, 2s. 6d. The Cottage Edition, 32mo, sewed, 8d. The Same, cloth, gilt edges, 1s. 6d. Another Edition, with Illustrations by Birket Foster and others, fcap., gilt cloth, 3s. 6d., or with edges gilt, 4s.
PORT ROYAL LOGIC. Translated from the French: with Introduction, Notes, and Appendix. By THOMAS SPENCER BAYNES, LL.D., Professor in the University of St Andrews. Eighth Edition, 12mo, 4s.
POTTS AND DARNELL. Aditus Faciliores: An easy Latin Construing Book, with Complete Vocabulary. By A. W. POTTS, M.A., LL.D., Head-Master of the Fettes College, Edinburgh, and sometime Fellow of St John's College, Cambridge; and the Rev. C. DARNELL, M.A., Head-Master of Cargilfield Preparatory School, Edinburgh, and late Scholar of Pembroke and Downing Colleges, Cambridge. Ninth Edition, fcap. 8vo, 3s. 6d.
—— Aditus Faciliores Graeci. An easy Greek Construing Book, with Complete Vocabulary. Third Edition, fcap. 8vo, 3s.
PRINGLE. The Live-Stock of the Farm. By ROBERT O. PRINGLE. Third Edition. Edited and Revised by JAMES MACDONALD, Editor of the 'Live-Stock Journal,' &c. Crown 8vo, 7s. 6d.
PRINGLE. A Journey in East Africa towards the Mountains of the Moon. By Mrs Pringle of Whytbank, Yair. New Edition. With a Map, 8vo, 5s.
PUBLIC GENERAL STATUTES AFFECTING SCOTLAND, from 1707 to 1847, with Chronological Table and Index. 3 vols. large 8vo, £3, 3s.
PUBLIC GENERAL STATUTES AFFECTING SCOTLAND, COLLECTION OF. Published Annually with General Index.
RAMSAY. Rough Recollections of Military Service and Society. By Lieut.-Col. BALCARRES D. WARDLAW RAMSAY. Two vols. post 8vo, 21s.
RAMSAY. Scotland and Scotsmen in the Eighteenth Century. From the MSS. of JOHN RAMSAY, Esq. of Ochtertyre. In two vols. 8vo. [In the press.

RANKINE. A Treatise on the Rights and Burdens incident to the Ownership of Lands and other Heritages in Scotland. By JOHN RANKINE, M.A., Advocate. Second Edition, Revised and Enlarged. 8vo, 45s.

RECORDS OF THE TERCENTENARY FESTIVAL OF THE UNIVERSITY OF EDINBURGH. Celebrated in April 1884. Published under the Sanction of the Senatus Academicus. Large 4to, £2, 12s. 6d.

RIMMER. The Early Homes of Prince Albert. By ALFRED RIMMER, Author of 'Our Old Country Towns,' &c. Beautifully Illustrated with Tinted Plates and numerous Engravings on Wood. 8vo, 21s.

ROBERTSON. Orellana, and other Poems. By J. LOGIE ROBERTSON, M.A. Fcap. 8vo. Printed on hand-made paper. 6s.

——— The White Angel of the Polly Ann, and other Stories. A Book of Fables and Fancies. Fcap. 8vo, 3s. 6d.

——— Our Holiday Among the Hills. By JAMES and JANET LOGIE ROBERTSON. Fcap. 8vo, 3s. 6d.

ROSCOE. Rambles with a Fishing-rod. By E. S. ROSCOE. Crown 8vo, 4s. 6d.

ROSS. Old Scottish Regimental Colours. By ANDREW ROSS, S.S.C., Hon. Secretary Old Scottish Regimental Colours Committee. Dedicated by Special Permission to Her Majesty the Queen. Folio, handsomely bound in cloth, £2, 12s. 6d.

RUSSELL. The Haigs of Bemersyde. A Family History. By JOHN RUSSELL. Large 8vo, with Illustrations. 21s.

RUSTOW. The War for the Rhine Frontier, 1870: Its Political and Military History. By Col. W. RUSTOW. Translated from the German, by JOHN LAYLAND NEEDHAM, Lieutenant R.M. Artillery. 3 vols. 8vo, with Maps and Plans, £1, 11s. 6d.

SCOTCH LOCH FISHING. By "Black Palmer." Crown 8vo, interleaved with blank pages, 4s.

SELLER AND STEPHENS. Physiology at the Farm; in Aid of Rearing and Feeding the Live Stock. By WILLIAM SELLER, M.D., F.R.S.E., Fellow of the Royal College of Physicians, Edinburgh, formerly Lecturer on Materia Medica and Dietetics; and HENRY STEPHENS, F.R.S.E., Author of ' The Book of the Farm,' &c. Post 8vo, with Engravings, 16s.

SETON. Memoir of Alexander Seton, Earl of Dunfermline, Seventh President of the Court of Session, and Lord Chancellor of Scotland. By GEORGE SETON, M.A. Oxon.; Author of the 'Law and Practice of Heraldry in Scotland,' &c. Crown 4to, 21s.

SETH. Scottish Philosophy. A Comparison of the Scottish and German Answers to Hume. Balfour Philosophical Lectures, University of Edinburgh. By ANDREW SETH, M.A., Professor of Logic and Philosophy in the University College of South Wales and Monmouthshire. Crown 8vo, 5s.

SHADWELL. The Life of Colin Campbell, Lord Clyde. Illustrated by Extracts from his Diary and Correspondence. By Lieutenant-General SHADWELL, C.B. 2 vols. 8vo. With Portrait, Maps, and Plans. 36s.

SHAND. Fortune's Wheel. By ALEX. INNES SHAND, Author of 'Against Time,' &c. Originally published in 'Blackwood's Magazine.' 3 vols. post 8vo, 25s. 6d.

——— Letters from the West of Ireland. Reprinted from the 'Times.' Crown 8vo, 5s.

SHARPE. The Correspondence of Charles Kirkpatrick Sharpe. With a Memoir. In two vols. 8vo. Illustrated with Etchings and other Engravings. [In the press.

SIM. Margaret Sim's Cookery. With an Introduction by L. B. WALFORD, Author of 'Mr Smith: A Part of His Life,' &c. Crown 8vo, 5s.

SIMPSON. Dogs of other Days: Nelson and Puck. By EVE BLANTYRE SIMPSON. Fcap. 8vo, with Illustrations, 2s. 6d.

SKENE. A Strange Inheritance. By F. M. F. SKENE, Author of 'Hidden Depths.' 3 vols. post 8vo, 25s. 6d.

SMITH. Italian Irrigation: A Report on the Agricultural Canals of Piedmont and Lombardy, addressed to the Hon. the Directors of the East India Company; with an Appendix, containing a Sketch of the Irrigation System of Northern and Central India. By Lieut.-Col. R. BAIRD SMITH, F.G.S., Captain, Bengal Engineers. Second Edition. 2 vols. 8vo, with Atlas, 30s.

SMITH. Thorndale; or, The Conflict of Opinions. By WILLIAM SMITH, Author of 'A Discourse on Ethics,' &c. A New Edition. Crown 8vo, 10s. 6d.

—— Gravenhurst; or, Thoughts on Good and Evil. Second Edition, with Memoir of the Author. Crown 8vo, 8s.

SMITH. Greek Testament Lessons for Colleges, Schools, and Private Students, consisting chiefly of the Sermon on the Mount and the Parables of our Lord. With Notes and Essays. By the Rev. J. HUNTER SMITH, M.A., King Edward's School, Birmingham. Crown 8vo, 6s.

SMITH. Writings by the Way. By JOHN CAMPBELL SMITH, M.A., Sheriff-Substitute. Crown 8vo, 9s.

SMITH. The Secretary for Scotland. Being a Statement of the Powers and Duties of the new Scottish Office. With a Short Historical Introduction and numerous references to important Administrative Documents. By W. C. SMITH, LL.B., Advocate. 8vo, 6s.

SOLTERA. A Lady's Ride Across Spanish Honduras. By MARIA SOLTERA. With Illustrations. Post 8vo, 12s. 6d.

SORLEY. The Ethics of Naturalism. Being the Shaw Fellowship Lectures, 1884. By W. R. Sorley, M.A., Fellow of Trinity College, Cambridge, and Examiner in Philosophy in the University of Edinburgh. Crown 8vo, 6s.

SPEEDY. Sport in the Highlands and Lowlands of Scotland with Rod and Gun. By TOM SPEEDY. With Illustrations by Lieut.-General Hope Crealocke, C.B., C.M.G., and others. 8vo, 15s.

SPROTT. The Worship and Offices of the Church of Scotland; or, the Celebration of Public Worship, the Administration of the Sacraments, and other Divine Offices, according to the Order of the Church of Scotland. By GEORGE W. SPROTT, D.D., Minister of North Berwick. Crown 8vo, 6s.

STARFORTH. Villa Residences and Farm Architecture: A Series of Designs. By JOHN STARFORTH, Architect. 102 Engravings. Second Edition, medium 4to, £2, 17s. 6d.

STATISTICAL ACCOUNT OF SCOTLAND. Complete, with Index, 15 vols. 8vo, £16, 16s.
Each County sold separately, with Title, Index, and Map, neatly bound in cloth, forming a very valuable Manual to the Landowner, the Tenant, the Manufacturer, the Naturalist, the Tourist, &c.

STEPHENS. The Book of the Farm; detailing the Labours of the Farmer, Farm-Steward, Ploughman, Shepherd, Hedger, Farm-Labourer, Field-Worker, and Cattleman. By HENRY STEPHENS, F.R.S.E. Illustrated with Portraits of Animals painted from the life; and with 557 Engravings on Wood, representing the principal Field Operations, Implements, and Animals treated of in the Work. A New and Revised Edition, the third, in great part Rewritten. 2 vols. large 8vo, £3, 10s.

—— The Book of Farm Buildings; their Arrangement and Construction. By HENRY STEPHENS, F.R.S.E., Author of 'The Book of the Farm;' and ROBERT SCOTT BURN. Illustrated with 1045 Plates and Engravings. Large 8vo, uniform with 'The Book of the Farm,' &c. £1, 11s. 6d.

—— The Book of Farm Implements and Machines. By J. SLIGHT and R. SCOTT BURN, Engineers. Edited by HENRY STEPHENS. Large 8vo, uniform with 'The Book of the Farm,' £2, 2s.

—— Catechism of Practical Agriculture. With Engravings. 1s.

Hymenomycetes Britannici.
STEVENSON. British Fungi. (Hymenomycetes.) By Rev. JOHN STEVENSON, Author of 'Mycologia Scotia,' Hon. Sec. Cryptogamic Society of Scotland. 2 vols. post 8vo, with Illustrations. Vol. I. AGARICUS—BOLBITIUS, 12s. 6d. Vol. II. CORTINARIUS—DACRYMYCES.

STEWART. Advice to Purchasers of Horses. By JOHN STEWART, V.S., Author of 'Stable Economy.' 2s. 6d.
—— Stable Economy. A Treatise on the Management of Horses in relation to Stabling, Grooming, Feeding, Watering, and Working. By JOHN STEWART, V.S. Seventh Edition, fcap. 8vo, 6s. 6d.

STONE. Hugh Moore: a Novel. By EVELYN STONE. 2 vols. crown 8vo, 17s.

STORMONTH. Etymological and Pronouncing Dictionary of the English Language. Including a very Copious Selection of Scientific Terms. For Use in Schools and Colleges, and as a Book of General Reference. By the Rev. JAMES STORMONTH. The Pronunciation carefully Revised by the Rev. P. H. PHELP, M.A. Cantab. Eighth Edition, Revised throughout. Crown 8vo, pp. 800. 7s. 6d.
—— Dictionary of the English Language, Pronouncing, Etymological, and Explanatory. Revised by the Rev. P. H. PHELP. Library Edition. Imperial 8vo, handsomely bound in half morocco, 31s. 6d.
—— The School Etymological Dictionary and Word-Book. Combining the advantages of an ordinary pronouncing School Dictionary and an Etymological Spelling-book. Fcap. 8vo, pp. 254. 2s.

STORY. Nero; A Historical Play. By W. W. STORY, Author of 'Roba di Roma.' Fcap. 8vo, 6s.
—— Vallombrosa. Post 8vo, 5s.
—— He and She; or, A Poet's Portfolio. Fcap. 8vo, in parchment, 3s. 6d.
—— Poems. 2 vols., fcap., 7s. 6d.
—— Fiammetta. A Summer Idyl. Crown 8vo, 7s. 6d.

STURGIS. John-a-Dreams. A Tale. By JULIAN STURGIS. New Edition, crown 8vo, 3s. 6d.
—— Little Comedies, Old and New. Crown 8vo, 7s. 6d.

SUTHERLAND. Handbook of Hardy Herbaceous and Alpine Flowers, for general Garden Decoration. Containing Descriptions, in Plain Language, of upwards of 1000 Species of Ornamental Hardy Perennial and Alpine Plants, adapted to all classes of Flower-Gardens, Rockwork, and Waters; along with Concise and Plain Instructions for their Propagation and Culture. By WILLIAM SUTHERLAND, Gardener to the Earl of Minto; formerly Manager of the Herbaceous Department at Kew. Crown 8vo, 7s. 6d.

TAYLOR. The Story of My Life. By the late Colonel MEADOWS TAYLOR, Author of 'The Confessions of a Thug,' &c. &c. Edited by his Daughter. New and cheaper Edition, being the Fourth. Crown 8vo, 6s.

TAYLOR. Wayfarers. By U. ASHWORTH TAYLOR. In two vols. crown 8vo. 17s.

TEMPLE. Lancelot Ward, M.P. A Love-Story. By GEORGE TEMPLE. Crown 8vo. 7s. 6d.

THOLUCK. Hours of Christian Devotion. Translated from the German of A. Tholuck, D.D., Professor of Theology in the University of Halle. By the Rev. ROBERT MENZIES, D.D. With a Preface written for this Translation by the Author. Second Edition, crown 8vo, 7s. 6d.

THOMSON. Handy Book of the Flower-Garden: being Practical Directions for the Propagation, Culture, and Arrangement of Plants in Flower-Gardens all the year round. Embracing all classes of Gardens, from the largest to the smallest. With Engraved and Coloured Plans, illustrative of the various systems of Grouping in Beds and Borders. By DAVID THOMSON, Gardener to his Grace the Duke of Buccleuch, K.G., at Drumlanrig. Third Edition, crown 8vo, 7s. 6d.
—— The Handy Book of Fruit-Culture under Glass: being a series of Elaborate Practical Treatises on the Cultivation and Forcing of Pines, Vines, Peaches, Figs, Melons, Strawberries, and Cucumbers. With Engravings of Hothouses, &c., most suitable for the Cultivation and Forcing of these Fruits. Second Edition. Crown 8vo, with Engravings, 7s. 6d.

THOMSON. A Practical Treatise on the Cultivation of the Grape-Vine. By WILLIAM THOMSON, Tweed Vineyards. Tenth Edition, 8vo, 5s.

THOMSON. Cookery for the Sick and Convalescent. With Directions for the Preparation of Poultices, Fomentations, &c. By BARBARA THOMSON, Clovenfords. Fcap. 8vo, 1s. 6d.

TOM CRINGLE'S LOG. A New Edition, with Illustrations. Crown 8vo, cloth gilt, 5s. Cheap Edition, 2s.

TRANSACTIONS OF THE HIGHLAND AND AGRICULTURAL SOCIETY OF SCOTLAND. Published annually, price 5s.

TROLLOPE. An Autobiography by Anthony Trollope. Two Volumes, post 8vo, with Portrait. Second Edition. Price 21s.

——— The Fixed Period. 2 vols. fcap. 8vo, 12s.

——— An Old Man's Love. 2 vols. crown 8vo, 12s.

TULLOCH. Rational Theology and Christian Philosophy in England in the Seventeenth Century. By JOHN TULLOCH, D.D., Principal of St Mary's College in the University of St Andrews; and one of her Majesty's Chaplains in Ordinary in Scotland. Second Edition. 2 vols. 8vo, 16s.

——— Modern Theories in Philosophy and Religion. 8vo, 15s.

——— The Christian Doctrine of Sin ; being the Croall Lecture for 1876. Crown 8vo, 6s.

——— Theism. The Witness of Reason and Nature to an All-Wise and Beneficent Creator. 8vo, 10s. 6d.

——— Luther, and other Leaders of the Reformation. Third Edition, enlarged. Crown 8vo, 3s. 6d.

TWO STORIES OF THE SEEN AND THE UNSEEN. 'THE OPEN DOOR,' 'OLD LADY MARY.' Crown 8vo, cloth, 2s. 6d.

VEITCH. Institutes of Logic. By JOHN VEITCH, LL.D., Professor of Logic and Rhetoric in the University of Glasgow. Post 8vo, 12s. 6d.

VIRGIL. The Æneid of Virgil. Translated in English Blank Verse by G. K. RICKARDS, M.A., and Lord RAVENSWORTH. 2 vols. fcap. 8vo, 10s.

WADE. General Gordon's Share in the Crisis at Pekin, 1880. A Letter to Sir Henry Gordon, K.C.B., Author of 'Events in the Life of Charles George Gordon.' By Sir THOMAS FRANCIS WADE, K.C.B., Sometime H.M. Minister in China. 1 vol. crown 8vo. [In the press.

WALFORD. The Novels of L. B. WALFORD. New and Uniform Edition. Crown 8vo, each 5s.

MR SMITH: A PART OF HIS LIFE.	TROUBLESOME DAUGHTERS.
COUSINS.	DICK NETHERBY.
PAULINE.	THE BABY'S GRANDMOTHER.
HISTORY OF A WEEK.	

——— Nan, and other Stories. 2 vols. crown 8vo, 12s.

WARDEN. Poems. By FRANCIS HEYWOOD WARDEN. With a Notice by Dr Vanroth. Crown 8vo, 5s.

WARREN'S (SAMUEL) WORKS. People's Edition, 4 vols. crown 8vo, cloth, 15s. 6d. Or separately:—

Diary of a Late Physician. Cloth, 2s. 6d.; boards, 2s. Illustrated, crown 8vo, 7s. 6d.

Ten Thousand A-Year. Cloth, 3s. 6d.; boards, 2s. 6d.

Now and Then. The Lily and the Bee. Intellectual and Moral Development of the Present Age. 4s. 6d.

Essays: Critical, Imaginative, and Juridical. 5s.

WARREN. The Five Books of the Psalms. With Marginal Notes. By Rev. SAMUEL L. WARREN, Rector of Esher, Surrey; late Fellow, Dean, and Divinity Lecturer, Wadham College, Oxford. Crown 8vo, 5s.

WATSON. Christ's Authority ; and other Sermons. By the late ARCHIBALD WATSON, D.D., Minister of the Parish of Dundee, and one of Her Majesty's Chaplains for Scotland. With Introduction by the Very Rev. PRINCIPAL CAIRD, Glasgow. Crown 8vo, 7s. 6d.

WEBSTER. The Angler and the Loop-Rod. By DAVID WEBSTER. Crown 8vo, with Illustrations, 7s. 6d.

WELLINGTON. Wellington Prize Essays on "the System of Field Manœuvres best adapted for enabling our Troops to meet a Continental Army." Edited by Lieut.-General Sir EDWARD BRUCE HAMLEY, K.C.B. 8vo, 12s. 6d.

WESTMINSTER ASSEMBLY. Minutes of the Westminster Assembly, while engaged in preparing their Directory for Church Government, Confession of Faith, and Catechisms (November 1644 to March 1649). Edited by the Rev. Professor ALEX. T. MITCHELL, of St Andrews, and the Rev. JOHN STRUTHERS, LL.D. With a Historical and Critical Introduction by Professor Mitchell. 8vo, 15s.

WHITE. The Eighteen Christian Centuries. By the Rev. JAMES WHITE. Seventh Edition, post 8vo, with Index, 6s.

—— History of France, from the Earliest Times. Sixth Thousand, post 8vo, with Index, 6s.

WHITE. Archæological Sketches in Scotland—Kintyre and Knapdale. By Colonel T. P. WHITE, R.E., of the Ordnance Survey. With numerous Illustrations. 2 vols. folio, £4, 4s. Vol. I., Kintyre, sold separately, £2, 2s.

—— The Ordnance Survey of Great Britain. A Popular Account. 1 vol. post 8vo. [*In the press.*

WILLS AND GREENE. Drawing-room Dramas for Children. By W. G. WILLS and the Hon. Mrs GREENE. Crown 8vo, 6s.

WILSON. Works of Professor Wilson. Edited by his Son-in-Law, Professor FERRIER. 12 vols. crown 8vo, £2, 8s.

—— Christopher in his Sporting-Jacket. 2 vols., 8s.

—— Isle of Palms, City of the Plague, and other Poems. 4s.

—— Lights and Shadows of Scottish Life, and other Tales. 4s.

—— Essays, Critical and Imaginative. 4 vols., 16s.

—— The Noctes Ambrosianæ. 4 vols., 16s.

—— The Comedy of the Noctes Ambrosianæ. By CHRISTOPHER NORTH. Edited by JOHN SKELTON, Advocate. With a Portrait of Professor Wilson and of the Ettrick Shepherd, engraved on Steel. Crown 8vo, 7s. 6d.

—— Homer and his Translators, and the Greek Drama. Crown 8vo, 4s.

WILSON. From Korti to Khartum: A Journal of the Desert March from Korti to Gubat and of the Ascent of the Nile in General Gordon's Steamers. By Colonel Sir CHARLES W. WILSON, K.C.B., K.C.M.G., R.E. Seventh Edition. Crown 8vo, 2s. 6d.

WINGATE. Annie Weir, and other Poems. By DAVID WINGATE. Fcap. 8vo, 5s.

—— Lily Neil. A Poem. Crown 8vo, 4s. 6d.

WORDSWORTH. The Historical Plays of Shakspeare. With Introductions and Notes. By CHARLES WORDSWORTH, D.C.L., Bishop of S. Andrews. 3 vols. post 8vo, each price 7s. 6d.

—— A Discourse on Scottish Church History. From the Reformation to the Present Time. With Prefatory Remarks on the St Giles' Lectures, and Appendix of Notes and References. Crown 8vo, cloth, 2s. 6d.

WORSLEY. Poems and Translations. By PHILIP STANHOPE WORSLEY, M.A. Edited by EDWARD WORSLEY. Second Edition, enlarged. Fcap. 8vo, 6s.

WYLDE. An Ill-Regulated Mind. A Novel. By KATHARINE WYLDE, Author of 'A Dreamer.' Crown 8vo, 7s. 6d.

YOUNG. Songs of Béranger done into English Verse. By WILLIAM YOUNG. New Edition, revised. Fcap. 8vo, 4s. 6d.

YULE. Fortification: for the Use of Officers in the Army, and Readers of Military History. By Col. YULE, Bengal Engineers. 8vo, with numerous Illustrations, 10s. 6d.

Trieste Publishing has a massive catalogue of classic book titles. Our aim is to provide readers with the highest quality reproductions of fiction and non-fiction literature that has stood the test of time. The many thousands of books in our collection have been sourced from libraries and private collections around the world.

The titles that Trieste Publishing has chosen to be part of the collection have been scanned to simulate the original. Our readers see the books the same way that their first readers did decades or a hundred or more years ago. Books from that period are often spoiled by imperfections that did not exist in the original. Imperfections could be in the form of blurred text, photographs, or missing pages. It is highly unlikely that this would occur with one of our books. Our extensive quality control ensures that the readers of Trieste Publishing's books will be delighted with their purchase. Our staff has thoroughly reviewed every page of all the books in the collection, repairing, or if necessary, rejecting titles that are not of the highest quality. This process ensures that the reader of one of Trieste Publishing's titles receives a volume that faithfully reproduces the original, and to the maximum degree possible, gives them the experience of owning the original work.

We pride ourselves on not only creating a pathway to an extensive reservoir of books of the finest quality, but also providing value to every one of our readers. Generally, Trieste books are purchased singly - on demand, however they may also be purchased in bulk. Readers interested in bulk purchases are invited to contact us directly to enquire about our tailored bulk rates. Email: customerservice@triestepublishing.com

You May Also Like

Beardslee on Wrought-Iron and Chain-Cables. Experiments on the Strength of Wrought-Iron and of Chain-Cables

L. A. Beardslee & William Kent

ISBN: 9781760579739
Paperback: 138 pages
Dimensions: 6.14 x 0.30 x 9.21 inches
Language: eng

On the Laws and Practice of Horse Racing

Henry John Rous

ISBN: 9780649662401
Paperback: 198 pages
Dimensions: 6.14 x 0.42 x 9.21 inches
Language: eng

www.triestepublishing.com

You May Also Like

A Place of Repentance; Or, an Account of the London Colonial Training Institution and Ragged Dormitiry, for the Reformation of Youthful and Adult Male Criminals, Great Smith Street, Westminster

Samuel Martin

ISBN: 9780649059638
Paperback: 124 pages
Dimensions: 6.14 x 0.26 x 9.21 inches
Language: eng

The Essentials of Method. A Discussion of the Essential Form of Right Methods in Teaching. Observation, Generalization, Application

Charles DeGarmo

ISBN: 9780649577453
Paperback: 154 pages
Dimensions: 6.0 x 0.33 x 9.0 inches
Language: eng

www.triestepublishing.com

You May Also Like

ISBN: 9780649438075
Paperback: 116 pages
Dimensions: 5.5 x 0.24 x 8.25 inches
Language: eng

Abraham Lincoln: The Practical Mystic

Francis Grierson

ISBN: 9780649314775
Paperback: 70 pages
Dimensions: 6.14 x 0.14 x 9.21 inches
Language: eng

A brief history of political parties in the United States

J. L. Pickard

www.triestepublishing.com

You May Also Like

A Calendar of Sonnets

Helen Jackson

ISBN: 9780649265701
Paperback: 60 pages
Dimensions: 6.14 x 0.12 x 9.21 inches
Language: eng

A Calendar of Sonnets

Helen Jackson

ISBN: 9780649323432
Paperback: 64 pages
Dimensions: 6.14 x 0.13 x 9.21 inches
Language: eng

Find more of our titles on our website. We have a selection of thousands of titles that will interest you. Please visit

www.triestepublishing.com

Lightning Source UK Ltd.
Milton Keynes UK
UKHW02f0820100718
325485UK00008B/758/P